PENGUIN BOOKS
AN OPEN WINDOW

Sri Madhava Ashish (1920–1997), who was for many years the head of a remote ashram, Mirtola, in the Kumaon hills of northern India, was a spiritual teacher whose teachings transcend conventional religious categories.

Born in Edinburgh, Sri Madhava Ashish was trained as an aircraft engineer in London and came to India during the Second World War. While travelling in India after the war, he met the great sage Ramana Maharshi at Tiruvannamalai and realized the supreme importance of the inner quest. His search led him to Mirtola ashram and to his guru, Sri Krishna Prem, an English professor who had become a Vaishnava monk.

At Sri Krishna Prem's death, nearly twenty years later, Sri Madhava Ashish became the head of the ashram and with his successor, Dev Ashish, he transformed the ashram farm and forest, making it a model for environmentally sound rural development. He served on several Planning Commission committees for hill development, and was awarded the Padma Shri by the Government of India in 1992 for his work on environmental education.

In his teachings, Sri Madhava Ashish integrated tradition and modern thought, eastern wisdom and western analysis. He wrote a number of articles and books for international publications.

An Open Window

Dream as Everyman's Guide to the Spirit

SRI MADHAVA ASHISH

PENGUIN BOOKS

PENGUIN BOOKS
Published by the Penguin Group
Penguin Books India Pvt. Ltd, 11 Community Centre, Panchsheel Park,
New Delhi 110 017, India
Penguin Group (USA) Inc., 375 Hudson Street, New York, New York 10014, USA
Penguin Group (Canada), 90 Eglinton Avenue East, Suite 700, Toronto, M4P 2Y3
(a division of Pearson Penguin Canada Inc.)
Penguin Books Ltd, 80 Strand, London WC2R 0RL, England
Penguin Ireland, 25 St Stephen's Green, Dublin 2, Ireland (a division of Penguin
Books Ltd)
Penguin Group (Australia), 250 Camberwell Road, Camberwell, Victoria 3124,
Australia (a division of Pearson Australia Group Pty Ltd)
Penguin Group (NZ), 67 Apollo Drive, Rosedale, North Shore 0632, New
Zealand (a division of Pearson New Zealand Ltd)
Penguin Group (South Africa) (Pty) Ltd, 24 Sturdee Avenue, Rosebank,
Johannesburg 2196, South Africa

Penguin Books Ltd, Registered Offices: 80 Strand, London WC2R 0RL, England

First published in India by Penguin Books India 2007

Copyright © Sri Dev Ashish 2007

10 9 8 7 6 5 4 3

ISBN-13: 978-0-14310-023-2   ISBN-10: 0-14310-023-8

Typeset in Sabon by Mantra Virtual Services, New Delhi
Printed at Chaman Offset Printers, Delhi

Contents

Foreword

It is indeed a windfall to get hold of Sri Madhava Ashishji's writings on dream interpretation. This represents an invaluable treasure trove of insights into the fascinating adventure of grasping the significance of dreams. In fact, dream interpretation represented a major facet of the teachings of Sri Krishna Prem and Sri Madhava Ashish, and in the book of their letters to me (*Letters from Mirtola*, Bharatiya Vidya Bhavan, 2004) there are numerous references to various dreams and their interpretation.

Although this process was originated by Sigmund Freud and developed in depth by Carl Gustav Jung, the Mirtola approach was unique. Creative dream interpretation throws light upon many dark aspects of the human psyche which are suppressed by our conscious mind and often manifest themselves in undesirable and unpleasant outer events. Dreams provide a searchlight which can be turned upon these dark areas, bringing them into the light of consciousness, there to be dealt with. Often enough what comes up is not at all pleasant or reassuring. Indeed, it usually involves facing up to certain parts of our emotional life which we are normally reluctant to do. However, movement on the spiritual path necessarily involves taking light into the dark corners of our psyche, and it is there that dreams provide an open window into the inner reality.

As Sri Madhava Ashish writes in one of his letters to me: 'Regarding the psychological interpretation of dreams, the whole significance turns on their being outside the range of the working of one's normal conscious integration. First, one has to understand what the human themes of universal application are: loves, hates, envies, greeds and ambitions. Then one has to take it on trust that a universal theme must have its individual application, and be ready to search for it with the certainty that it must be there. If it were easily visible and available to cursory examination, it would not be "unconscious". The material in this type of dream shows us ourselves "with the lid off". When one has done this sort of inner searching one becomes aware of how much of what seems free choice of action was in fact a predetermined pattern—determined by unrecognized subconscious drives and desires. Freedom from these desires and compulsions is the beginning of liberation.'

Apart from general observations regarding dream interpretation, Ashishda's book covers such diverse topics as Traumas, Anxiety, Social Conditioning, Reincarnation, Death Dreams and Great Beings. He also lays down seven Principles of Interpretation which encapsulate his insights in this field. This book will, therefore, be of tremendous value not only to professional psychologists but also to all those who are on the spiritual path. It is a privilege for me to write a brief foreword for this publication which, I hope, will be widely circulated in India and around the world.

Deepavali   Karan Singh
1 November 2005

Introduction

Sri Sri Madhava Ashish, Ashishda to his friends and disciples, was born in an aristocratic Scottish family on 23 February 1920 and christened Alexander Phipps. After a public school education, he graduated as an aircraft engineer from the Chelsea College of Aeronautical Engineering in London and came to India in 1942 as part of the ongoing war effort. After the war he took time off to see the country. At the Raman Ashram in Tiruvannamalai he had a wonderful darshan of the sage and an intense, crucial experience. Ashishda had no knowledge of Tamil but the Maharishi did not need the medium of language to give him 'the taste of the thing'—what is referred to in mystical literature as the Kundalini experience. By no means did that bring about the instant transformation of Alexander Phipps Esq. into Sri Sri Madhava Ashish. 'I still persisted in my youthful follies,' he said once, referring to that visit. But something crucial had happened. The seed had been sown. Or, perhaps more appropriately, the seed buried deep down had received the nourishing touch of living waters.

He did not need to wander across the country very long after that. Within a few months, he arrived at a small Vaishnava ashram in a village deep in the Kumaon hills of northern India where he found his guru and guide. Here began Ashishda's integration into the life of the spirit under the guidance of Sri Krishna Prem and Moti Rani, daughter of Yashoda Mai who had founded the ashram and its temple dedicated to Krishna. Together they put him through the paces. While the guru, endowed with a razor-sharp mind, phenomenal memory and a great flow of feelings taught in his own way, Moti Rani in her inimitable style created conditions and opportunities for practising and integrating the teaching. 'Thakur caught me by the scruff of the neck and brought me here' is how Ashishda once summarized the circumstances that had conspired to lead him to the place where he spent the rest of his life.

The transformation of an upper-class Englishman into a Vaishnava vairagi sadhu could not possibly have been without considerable suffering. He bore it with characteristic dedication and the doggedness required in an enterprise that involves, in T.S. Eliot's phrase, 'not less than everything'. Working like a horse and suffering the stormy upheavals that constituted Moti Rani's method of helping the 'work', Ashishda reached a stage once when he felt that he could take it no longer. That evening when he went to massage her feet, the last chore of his tiring day, he had made up his mind to leave the ashram quietly next morning. As he was tiptoeing out of the room, the apparently sleeping beneficiary of the massage remarked, 'So you will go away tomorrow without even saying goodbye to me!' Result: he stayed on. Moti Rani was utterly devoted to the path of selfless service and, like H.P. Blavatsky, freely used her gift of occult powers to help deserving seekers.

His personal sadhana included a very rigorous regimen: austerities, hard physical work, study, temple rituals, meditation, and above all, intelligent inquiry, for which he had a special flair. One can see in this picture all the textbook ingredients of spiritual striving within the traditions of Hinduism—shraddha, jigyasa, yam, niyam, dhyan, swadhyay, vichar, sumiran, sewa (faith, inquiry, self-restraint, observances, meditation, self-study, pondering, remembrance, service)—the whole works! And no wonder—he had his own reasons to believe, as he has said in this book, that he had been a Hindu sadhu in more than one of his past lives. It is, however, also possible to describe his 'work' in Gurdjieffian, Buddhist, Sufi or Theosophical terms. Labels apart, slowly and steadily things were working out. 'Clench your teeth and stick it out,' Sri Krishna Prem had advised a fellow traveller, 'we have no past.' Ashishda stuck it out bravely and as for not having a past, he once told a friend casually that the word 'mother' did not bring to his mind the figure of the mother he was born of. A confirmation of this could be seen in his beatific smile when he recited his favourite Sanskrit hymn that begins: 'My mother is Parvati and father Shiva. His devotees are my kin and his kingdom my country.'

After his guru's passing away in 1965, he had to fill the role not only of the Pradhan Sewak of the ashram but also that of friend, philosopher and guide to a number of friends and followers from India and abroad. He taught what he had learnt and integrated in himself—a teaching with Unity as its core doctrine and compassion its practice. Together they ruled out the quest for 'an everlasting personal bliss' that is the mainstay of many spiritual cults and lures many an earnest seeker. He kept up the subtle work, started by his guru, of simplifying the rituals and observances and highlighting their inner meaning so that instead of becoming hindrances they served as aids to graduate 'from the symbol to the thing symbolized'. Besides his 'regular' disciples, many others were drawn to him by the magic that they sensed and felt in his presence. That magic did not disappear with the death of his body on 13 April 1997.

It is unfair to deny to the guru, as some naive enthusiasts may be inclined to do, all attributes of ordinary humanity and place him on such a pedestal that there is no scope left to see 'the human in the numinous'. This kind of devotional posturing often collapses when they come face-to-face with some of the more unconventional sayings and doings of the teacher. Some start picking holes in the teaching, calling it a hotchpotch of Vaishnavism, Advaita, Buddhism, Sufi mysticism, Theosophy, Gurdjieffianism—with the additional confusion of 'this dream business'. It is indeed a rare brew, distilled from ingredients collected from regions far and wide, which defies classification.

Ashishda is known to have told some of his disciples that he was only a 'pupil–teacher' and this was not just the humility of a good sadhu. The path that he followed and of which he is a guide involves the surrender of personal salvation and a commitment to compassion—'having crossed over to the other shore he helps others to cross' as Shankaracharya put it.[1] Such a teacher has to continuously evolve, forever refining his capacity to help in the light of the changing outer situations in which he is required to work. He has to keep on learning as he teaches. For such pupil–teachers, it is not arriving but journeying that is important—'the road is the goal'.[2] This road of truly universal and secular spirituality extends 'from soil to soul' and encompasses the whole of life.

Besides extending and modernizing the ashram farm and dairy, Ashishda did pioneering work in the field of ecology

---

[1] *Vivek Churamani.*
[2] *I Am That*, Sri Nisargadatta Maharaj, Acorn Press, 1973.

and the environment to create awareness of the basic issues among schoolchildren and villagers. This led to some raised eyebrows. And when he accepted the Padma Shri award of the Government of India, there was even greater bafflement and surprise. What has all this to do with a Vaishnava sadhu, some people wondered. But then this same sadhu had sat on the dais of a political meeting held in a nearby village to protest against the state of Emergency that had been imposed by Indira Gandhi's government, thus declaring his moral support for the cause of democracy and freedom.

If working on oneself—climbing up the mountain path of spiritual striving—is tough, guiding others in the same enterprise is tougher. Ashishda went through considerable turmoil and suffering before reconciling himself to this role. Meeting and satisfying the curiosity of a growing number of ashram-hopping spiritual tourists was the least difficult part of it. The number of genuine seekers with different personal problems and degrees of earnestness also grew steadily. From them he held back nothing and gave freely, to each according to his or her need, from his vast treasure of earned and integrated Self-knowledge. He had no liking for formal speeches and discourse but he was always available for discussion and talk on general issues concerning the spiritual effort as well as specific personal problems. Such 'sessions' were very informal and not like closed-door meetings of a cult. Then he had to deal with numerous letters containing serious philosophical questions and often many dreams for interpretation. In recent years, four books[3] have been

---

[3] *Relating To Reality*, Sri Madhava Ashish; Banyan Books. *Guru By Your Bedside*, S.D. Pandey; Penguin, 2003. *In Search of the Unitive Vision*, Seymour B. Ginsburg; New Paradigm, 2001. *Letters from Mirtola*, Karan Singh; Bharatiya Vidya Bhavan, 2005.

published in which his letters have been compiled or quoted in detail. His major contribution to the realm of thought consists of the two books, *Man, the Measure of All Things*, co-authored with Sri Krishna Prem, and *Man, Son of Man*. They are commentaries on the *Stanzas of Dzyan* that are a part of H.P. Blavatsky's monumental mystical work, *The Secret Doctrine*. Put in intelligible language, the intricately coded knowledge condensed in these stanzas took him many years of hard work—pondering, wondering, thinking and trying to understand the hints and suggestions coming through dreams and intuitions.

This little 'dream' book was given its final shape during the last few years of Ashishda's life when he was suffering from a terminal illness. More than just another layman's guide to dream interpretation, it is a compressed monograph of his central teachings—a guide to the spirit. A letter that he wrote to an American disciple indicates his main approach to the subject. He wrote:

> Your inquiry about dreams is difficult to answer for the reason that I know of no book which handles dreams as a guide to the inner life. Every analyst seems to have his own views on the meaning of dreams, but they all appear to agree that social adaptation is the be-all and end-all of psychology.
>
> Even C.G. Jung with his archetypal dreams and collective unconscious, stops short of publicly admitting the independent reality of the Self. He slurs the point by admitting that it is real as a human experience, but avoids admitting that it is real in itself . . . .
>
> . . . any reading of psychology and related dream interpretation is valuable in so far as it throws light on the workings of the mind. But one has always to read with

caution . . . . One needs every bit of help one can get in learning the language of dreams. But it is difficult to learn the language without having a lot of psychological theories foisted on one, most theories being based on the assumption that the psyche's concern is with the current standards of normality.'

He further elaborated on this in a subsequent letter:

The psychological theory of dreaming has, of course, been popular since Freud. This still holds good. What is lacking in most current dream theory, as it is lacking in the current worldview, is the presence of a spiritual centre and a universal view to which the personal psychic patterns can be related, and which gives significance to the person and his or her struggles to understand the psyche.

Our difficulty lies in the fact that modern psychology has achieved remarkable insights into the working of the subconscious mind-feeling complex and the effects it has on the feelings and thoughts we are aware of. All this is of immense usefulness to anyone struggling to control his or her mind, and to deal with negative emotions.

But we cannot afford to use this knowledge without distinguishing it from the uses to which modern psychology puts it . . . .

In our field we can treat as fact Freud's dictum that dreams are the royal road into the subconscious, but we do not therefore have to accept Freud's theories about ego and id, etc., or to accept the academic flavour that dulls so much of his work. Freud did not discover dreams; he gave some structure to the area of (un)awareness from which dreams (and much of our compulsive behaviour) take their rise. Dreams and visions have provided seekers with data for their search since the beginning of time.

Our work is so difficult that we need every bit of help we can get. It really does not matter where or from whom we take help, provided that we have enough intelligence and a clear enough view of our goal to be able to take help that is consonant with our aim and to reject those components that are contrary to it.

It has to be emphasized that we need the tools, but not the men who fashioned these tools; they use them to help people who are so screwed up that they cannot even manage their daily lives; we intend to use them for liberating our minds from the compulsive forces which act on them.[4]

Under the increasing global influence of a materialist world view, one may be inclined to believe that all our personal and social problems pertain merely to an adjustment of outer circumstances and can be solved by suitable action in the areas of operation of politicians, economists, managers, doctors and psychologists. This little book should leave no doubt about the crucial role of spiritual work and guidance and the place of 'this dream business' in this regard.

Seymour B. Ginsburg and
Satish Datt Pandey

---

[4] *In Search of the Unitive Vision*, Seymour B. Ginsburg; New Paradigm, 2001.

Preface

This little book owes its existence to fifty years of spiritual discipline in which guidance from dreams played a crucial role. One must have dealt with thousands of one's own dreams, and thousands of the fifty or more people with whom we—my guru, Sri Krishna Prem, and I—were working. I had read a few of Freud's books before my guru introduced me to C.G. Jung, saying enigmatically: 'Read Jung, but don't become a Jungian. Read *The Secret of the Golden Flower*, but you needn't bother with Jung's preface.'

Interpretation was not restricted to dreams alone. My guru would read a man's history and character from the arrangement of his rooms, listen for the real questions behind the questioner's spoken presentations, and read behind the lines to assess an author's character, irrespective of what the book was about. Given this probing, analytical insight, the symbols of dream seldom made him pause. I feared his clarity, for too often he left me naked and ashamed, with all my hidden weaknesses exposed to view. How else could one discover that self-disgust which helps break the self-identification with one's pusillanimous youth.

As time went on and one learnt to enjoy the release from inhibitions, shame, guilt and fear, one began actively digging out repressed material instead of being the reluctant recipient of unwelcome messages. The nature of dream began to change. We went through a high period when a night without a dream was a wasted opportunity, a forgotten dream was a breach of trust. We hurried through our many chores to be free to pace up and down in the morning light, seeking meanings and their ramifications.

Then, as the mind began to come under control, little visions began to appear in meditation whose content was more direct, less concealed by symbols, than in ordinary dream.

There was direct, personal instruction. And there were dreams which threw light on the Cosmogenesis and Anthropogenesis of the *Stanzas of Dzyan*[1] on which we were writing a commentary. Yet there was never direct dictation. One always had to struggle to understand what the symbols were saying, so that one was personally responsible for the form in which the general scheme was presented. Often this involved challenging the sacred truths of received wisdom: if anything could not withstand the challenge, it had to go.

Out of all this came the realization that we were dealing with a view of the universe and its spiritual origins which, if we were honest, would make us examine and reformulate the religious teaching which had guided us so far. For we had been introduced to and brought up in a school of the orthodox Krishna cult. There were some things one just did not question, such as what one meant by Krishna. I was given an overwhelming vision of Radha-Krishna,[2] shining in all

---

[1] Verses of obscure origin, obtained by H.P. Blavatsky, the founder of the Theosophical Society, which formed the backbone of her great work, *The Secret Doctrine*.

[2] Krishna and his consort Radha are the archetypal lovers of Indian culture, just as Laila and Majnun are of the Persian, and Lancelot and Guinevere of the Arthurian legend.

their glory, and within a few days shown that this was the view of an immature boy. It was by no means the end of the path, as it had seemed to be, but only the beginning of a new stage on the road to the completion of the human task.

So slow is the pace of change at times that it took a long time before one could see how this 'new', almost secular approach to the truth could be reconciled with what were also the real truths of the devotional approach. *Omnia vincit amor* (love conquers all), the Vaishnava greeting *Jai Radhe* (victory to Radha) and Krishna as Prema Swarup (the self-nature of love) were all saying the same thing, and one did not need to get stuck with a particular image. The love which glues the universe together is utterly real and needs no peacock feathers, flutes, necklaces and caste marks to make it visible.

It all sounds so simple that one is almost ashamed to admit having found it so difficult to see. Yet I have known people ready to sneer at my simplicity who seemed to have understanding without love. And all sorts of people who agree with what I say yet still want the blessings of a mythical deity for their sons' success in school examinations.

The way I like to present it goes something like this: we find ourselves in this wonderful universe, full of living things that grow and decay—sensitive plants, intelligent animals, singing birds, roaring tigers, and caterpillars that metamorphose into butterflies. And then there are men: wonderful men and horrible men, crude and refined men, dull and brilliant men, the only living beings capable of formulating the question of where everything comes from and what it is all about.

As a man, if one were to ask these questions while ignoring the second-hand wisdom passed down to us, might one not arrive at the conclusion that the answer to the whole mystery must lie in the solution to the greatest mystery of all, namely, what is the nature of the awareness that allows one not only to observe this mysterious universe, but also to know that one observes it—to lie in the distinction between the observer himself and the biological apparatus of observation?

As soon as one begins this inquiry, one is faced with its root problem: what I seek at the root of my being by its very nature cannot be taken out and looked at, for it is itself the very thing that looks. Yet, like the mirror in which I can see my own face, there is a mirror that reflects many of the qualities of this unseeable source of awareness.

That mirror is dream. The more one cleans and polishes it, the more clearly it reflects. And though one must not confuse the brilliance of the mirror image with the incandescence of what it reflects, neither should one deny the validity of the knowledge it gives, for dream can turn to vision, and vision can turn to understanding.

Like any other approach to the mystery of being, dream work can take one only a certain distance along the road, to the point where the individual begins to be lost in the universal and the world reveals itself as the mirror of the creative ideation.

Mirtola   Sri Madhava Ashish

The Importance of Dreams

From time immemorial, mankind has found guidance in dreams. Dreams and visions have given insight into the nature of man and the universe, indications about the future, and communications with the dead. There were, and still are, temples dedicated to the gods of healing, where the sick might sleep until they received a dream which, interpreted by the priests, prescribed a treatment and gave a prognosis. Their reliability depended as much on the interpreter's skill, knowledge and intuitive capacity as it did on the dreamer's dream recall and truthfulness. To explain the difference between clear and opaque dreams, the Greeks suggested that true dreams came from the inner worlds through gates of horn—thin strips of translucent horn being used for windows before glass became available—while false dreams came through gates of opaque ivory.

Skilled interpreters were few and far between. Much interpretation was, therefore, on the level of folklore and superstition—rule of thumb interpretations, such as that a dream of eating is bad, while a dream of defecating is good, or that (in India) a dream of a marriage party means someone's death. It is not surprising that rationalism brushed away the science of dreams as 'old wives' tales'.

At the beginning of the twentieth century, Sigmund Freud

and other pioneers, developing depth psychology, realized that the images of dream often represent memories of emotionally charged events in the dreamer's life which have been repressed, or held under the threshold of waking consciousness, because they are too painful for the person to handle. Thus they were 'forgotten'; but such forgetting did not make them impotent. From their concealed position they continued to affect the person, often producing seemingly irrational behaviour of a compulsive nature. Interpretation of dreams could lead to recovery of these painful memories, with beneficial effects on the dreamer.

The value of dreams as throwing light on personal psychology was generally accepted, but prognostic and metaphysical dreams were still considered disreputable, in spite of the work of C.G. Jung, because they could find no place in the dominant world view which excludes all non-physical aspects of being from its framework of reference, and excludes precognition as indicating a quality of time which threatens the basis of scientific materialism.

Having succumbed to the materialist and rationalist world view, these modern psychological schools are automatically restricted to treating their patients as if successful adaptation to human society, as it is now, is the highest goal a human being can aspire to. It is, therefore, not surprising that many spiritual schools refuse to have anything to do with this sort of psychology. The leaders of the Gurdjieff groups, in particular, appear to have thrown the baby out with the bath water by discarding not only psychology but also dreams, because of a derogatory remark made about dreams by Mr Gurdjieff.[1] (This

---

[1] George Ivanovitch Gurdjieff (1866–1949), enigmatic spiritual master whose teachings transcend traditional religious categories and shaped some of the key elements of contemporary spirituality.

is curious. Whatever Mr Gurdjieff may have said, his behaviour implies the opposite. Several highly respected psychologists were his disciples, and they continued working with dreams. The evidence of Margaret Anderson[2] and Ethel Merston[3] is that Gurdjieff listened sympathetically to their dreams at the Prieuré.)

However, if we put such prejudice aside and examine the facts, we find not only that the ancient treatment of dream as a window into the inner worlds is valid, but also that the tools of modern psychology can be used to unlock the meanings of dream and so help us to free our minds and feelings from the compulsions and inhibitions which stem from unconscious determinants. This means that we have at our disposal the means to track down, identify and then free ourselves from the desires, fears, and insecurities which well up from below the threshold of the waking mind and give our thoughts their seemingly uncontrollable drive—turbulent thoughts which obstruct our efforts to quieten the mind in meditation.

In meditation, some thoughts can be brought under control by a simple act of will. But there are others which make us their captives and carry us off; if we stop them for a moment, they quickly start again. However, when we identify the subconscious forces which drive them, we can, as it were, turn off their energy supply, and they are tamed. Our meditation improves and, as a side benefit, our adaptation to life may also improve.

---

[2] *The Unknowable Gurdjieff,* Margaret Anderson; Routledge & Kegan Paul, 1962. Margaret Anderson was the founder of *The Little Review* and published the work of many writers who subsequently became famous, including T.S. Eliot, Ezra Pound, Hemingway and James Joyce.

[3] Ethel (or Esther) Merston. Personal communication.

Since we cannot hope to transcend the mind without passing beyond its surface, and one cannot get past the surface while it is churning with thoughts, we should welcome any means by which thoughts can be controlled. Indeed, it is remarkable that so many people who long for proof of a reality which is beyond the limits of the sensible universe pay no attention to this window open to non-physical levels of being. Is this because 'the Guardian of the Threshold' bars their entry? Put into ordinary language, this would mean that the first images to rise into dream from the threshold of consciousness are felt to be so frightening or so disgusting that the person either forgets the dream or is too ashamed to relate it. The most common subject of such dreams is sex, and that is why so much attention has to be given to it in the following pages.

But sex is by no means the only source of traumas and of manifestations of 'the Dweller on the Threshold', as the following story shows.

Nirmala, an Indian woman, came from a family of many brothers and sisters. She resented the gender discrimination, common to the social orthodoxy of the time, which gave considerable freedom to the boys to move about as they pleased, whereas the girls had to stay at home except when they went out with their parents. Nirmala wished she had been born a boy.

At some point in her youth, she learned about an Indian woman artist who, by virtue of her profession, lived an independent life, and she fantasized that she would become an artist and be independent. To this end she learned to paint, but she could not stop her father from marrying her off in the conventional fashion. However, her husband's circumstances permitted her the leisure to continue painting, and she achieved a certain competence.

After some years, both husband and wife started taking instruction from Sri Krishna Prem and myself, and our teaching included the use of psychology to clear the ground and bring the mind under control. Nirmala's dreams showed that her fantasy of becoming an independent woman artist needed attention, but she became impatient with this part of the work and declared that she would concentrate on meditation, even though her guru warned her against abandoning the psychological inquiry.

As it happens when meditation is pursued with enthusiasm, the inner eye of vision opened and she *saw*. What she saw was a ghost in her room—and she was terrified of ghosts. It was the ghost of a woman artist.

It was months before Nirmala dared meditate again.

2

Dreams and the Inner Inquiry

That great pioneer of modern psychology, Sigmund Freud, called dreams the royal road into the unconscious. To others it may seem to be more like one of those rough and rather eroded cow tracks one finds in high-altitude pastures. Royal or rough, however, this raises the question of what does lie below, behind or beyond the surface of the waking mind, and why anyone would want to go there.

Much lies there, both the memories we can summon up to consciousness and those which are too weak or too painful to come at our bidding. Deeper than those lie the memories of previous lives and, deeper still, the memory traces of an ancestry we may fairly call divine—Wordsworth's 'Trailing clouds of glory'.

In there are the means by which archetypal principles of being can find expression in the images of dream and vision. There we can come face-to-face with the gods—impersonal powers of life and consciousness. There too, the powers of the elements—gnomes, undines, sylphs, and salamanders—take on hominid characteristics.

This realm of dream is the realm of magic, myth and mystery. It is a fluid realm whose stability lies only in the observer, never in the images observed. It is a flexible realm which adapts itself to the needs of the dreamer. It is ambiguous, its messages yielding different meanings to different interpreters—and all capable of being true. By ordinary social standards it is amoral, yet when one passes deeper, one finds the very roots of true morality.

Dream interpreters in general, and psychologists in particular, are vulnerable to the charge that they interpret dreams to suit their own books. But it is also true that the dreaming power shapes its symbols to suit the interpreter. It is a common jibe that those who go to a Freudian analyst get Freudian dreams, while those who go to a Jungian get Jungian ones. Who or what does the shaping?

The truth behind this jibe is that the autonomous psyche will not cast its pearls of transcendental wisdom before an interpreter who, for example, can think only in terms of anal eroticism. But if the dreamer has such anal components in his make-up, the psyche may well present them for interpretation where they will be understood.

So the power that shapes the symbols, the artist of our dreams, is the Self, the Soul, the Atman: that strange autonomous being who both is and is not the person of our waking personalities. Some of us aim to discover whether this Self is real and not, as materialists would have us believe, an ephemeral illusion, born of brain activity and ceasing when it ceases. This search will lead us below the surface of the waking mind and into unmapped country.

When seeking an answer to this crucially human question, the dream is not only a royal road into psychology's seething cauldron of repressed sexuality, or even into the oceanic symbols of the collective unconscious. It is also, and more importantly, an open window into the inner kingdom of the Soul.

At this point we cannot ignore the common charge that since the belief in the existence of the soul is without rational foundation, unprovable in the terms of contemporary science, then all this talk about the Kingdom of the Soul is meaningless. Dreams can be, at the most, only random productions of the idling, computer-like brain.

Such an unprovable assumption against the existence of the Soul does not invalidate the opposite assumption of its existence. The denial is like that of a blind man who cannot understand how anyone could see.

To many people, therefore, the path of life seems to lie between precipitous cliffs of matter, on the one hand, and the unplumbed depths of the unconscious mind, on the other. It is paved with rock, for our lives have a material base, but what lies beneath the paving, whether matter or consciousness or nothing at all, is uncertain. We can overcome this dilemma by putting the question in strictly secular form, free from assumptions: Is there, or is there not, anything more than the world as perceived through the organs of sense? If so, have we any place in it as experiencing individuals? Can we then know its nature?

Putting the question in this form liberates our inquiry from the whole gamut of religious teachings, their associated mythologies and superstitions, their confirmations or denials by mystical visionaries, the speculations of philosophers and, of course, from the flat denials of the materialistic scientists. Why it liberates needs explanation.

As soon as we have formulated our inquiry in terms of a 'something more' which is outside the limited scope of the sense organs' range of perception, we are thrown back onto whatever it is that observes and then interprets the electro-magnetic or electrochemical messages supplied to the brain by the organs of sense.

Whatever this may be, it is for each one of us our sole source of first-hand knowledge of the world. But when (through the sense organs) we receive accounts of what someone else claims either to have sensed, or to have perceived without the organs of sense, it is knowledge at second-hand. This second-hand knowledge may have some validity when it corresponds with our own first-hand experience, but as second-hand sense-organ information, it has neither validity nor relevance in the context of our inquiry, which, we have ourselves determined, is about something that cannot be perceived by the physical sense organs. We are, therefore, thrown back on our own capacity to perceive and interpret any mental content which is not coming immediately from the sense organs.

Let us suppose we find that our 'something more' exists and is perceptible through other avenues of perception than the physical organs, and let us suppose it corresponds to or agrees with religious, philosophical, and mystical teachings. Would this mean that our inquiry was unnecessary because we had merely rediscovered something that was already known? Ought we to have remained content with belief in (and doubt of) the traditional teachings? The answer is No.

A statement of fact about the sensible universe can be confirmed or denied by anyone using his sense organs in the prescribed manner, for the interpretation of sense data is remarkably uniform throughout the human population, and this is why we share the same world. But with respect to data not supplied by the sense organs and not necessarily related to the purely sensible universe, the relatively few people who experience them are likely to say something like: 'Only now do I have the foundation of experience which permits me to understand what so-and-so meant when he made that specific statement about non-physical states of being.' In other words, the new discoverer now shares a common ground of experience with the earlier discoverer, this making it possible for the two to understand each other.

The jibe that the two are merely sharing a hallucination is liable to backfire when it is appreciated that the human race's general agreement about the shape, colour, and texture of the world we perceive through the sense organs is due to the sharing of what might easily be a hallucination. Colourless electromagnetic vibrations of specific frequencies reflected from colourless surfaces strike the retina of the eye, which converts them to corresponding electrochemical impulses in the optic nerve. Those impulses then stimulate neurons in the brain.

At this point, a remarkable transformation occurs. Colourless impulses of measurable frequency give rise to the experience of colour in consciousness. The fact that there is a known correlation between a given frequency and the experienced colour does not excuse attempts to blur the issue that the observable frequencies are states of physical energies, while the experience of colour is a state of consciousness. (A.N. Whitehead called the first a 'neurosis'—a state of the nerves, and the second a 'psychosis'—a state of the psyche; he seems to have despaired of people who could not distinguish between these different orders of being.) Also, the probable fact that the computer-like activities of the brain assist in the 'compare and contrast' process of recognition and interpretation, including naming, in no way alters the fact that the step which follows the brain's mechanistic activity as a sorting device is a recognition in consciousness.

And so we come back to the Self, the Soul, the Atman: the Observer or Witness of all the data fed to the brain by the sense organs, the Keeper of our memories, the Ruler of the mind and its shimmering images.

Meditation is the means by which we can learn to identify the Self and to differentiate it from the everyday ego-centre. Dreams are everyone's window into the inner world of non-physical reality; through it comes the inspiration and guidance of our higher being. The related state of Vision, at its best, is a relatively undistorted state of seeing in which the absence of ego-reference is so marked that it is only after the return to normal consciousness that the person can say 'I saw'.

Put very briefly: when the mind has been brought to rest, then the Self stands in its own nature. All mental disturbances derive from the ego's hopes, fears, loves, hates, desires, aversions, anxieties, and insecurities. This is why the trans-egotistic Observer, Seer or Self cannot be isolated and discovered until these distorting influences have been put to rest. Putting them to rest requires that one traces them to their roots, understands them and ceases to fear them. Dreams frequently help us to make the necessary connections between the disturbing factors and their roots, thus breaking their compulsive power.

So our inquiry begins with the search for the Observer of sense stimuli and of the thoughts and feelings which arise from them, for it is the Observer's self-awareness—its awareness that it is aware of these images in consciousness—which gives us the sense of our having a permanent identity. We may seem to ourselves to be different people at different times, yet we are, or ought to be, aware that these different personas are masks worn by a nameless Self.

This self-aware Observer is at the root of the mystery of how a universe of seemingly inert energies is experienced in consciousness by sensitive, living, self-conscious beings who have evolved out of those 'inert' energies. Where all experience-based mystical teaching has described some sort of fundamental division between the experiencing Subject of the universe and the objective aspect of the universe, the whole being included within the total concept of consciousness, the materialistic scientists seem to believe that consciousness is an emergent property of energetic structures. This would mean that there is no observing Self, independent of the sense organs and brain, and that self-awareness is simply a function of neurones.

What appears to have happened here is that a false ascription of causal relations has been made: life is known to have appeared in connection with the creation of the highly complex DNA molecule. Therefore (it is falsely argued), life appeared as an emergent property of the atomic world, which required the peculiar complexity of the DNA molecule for it to become operative. Factually, life and consciousness have non-physical origins, it being closer to the mark to say that it was the ingression of life into an appropriate environment which produced the DNA molecule. The reason for the mistake is that both the DNA molecule and the atoms from which it is built are technically visible, while the living intelligence which informs the molecule, being of an entirely different order, is inherently invisible. To anyone committed to interpreting existence solely in terms of data supplied by the physical organs of sense, what is invisible does not exist. Therefore, it is argued, if something new appears, it has to have emerged from what was already visibly there.

It bears repeating that the first and most important task on this path of inner inquiry is the stilling of the mind. The screen onto which the mind projects its images can be likened to the surface of a mountain lake. So long as the surface is covered by waves and ripples, neither can we look down through the clear waters to see what lies beneath the surface, nor can the undistorted image of the heavens be reflected in the surface.

The ripples themselves can no more be held still than a flickering flame can be held with pincers. The winds which stir the ripples are our desires and fears; they have to be traced to their source, identified, and dealt with by a combination of disciplined control and intelligent analysis.

When this work is begun, the mind often appears so full of uncontrollable thoughts, so chaotic, that one does not know where to begin. As when given the task of unravelling a tangled ball of string, one starts by finding a loose end and proceeds from there, so the dreaming power will provide a starting point, leading one through the chaos until the mind is stilled. This is why dreams have been likened to Ariadne's thread of worsted by which Theseus, in Greek myth, found his way through the labyrinth of Minos.

The Self's power to give guidance through dreams is of profound significance, for it implies that the Self already knows the goal to which life is directed, and it is in this sense that the true guru is said to reside within the heart. In principle this is a straightforward derivation from the fact that the individualized Self is a spark of the universal fire of consciousness, so that the spark already embodies the knowledge of that unity which is the goal of human evolution, and can therefore guide us to its own state. However, this seems to clash with another important aspect of human evolution, expressed as the effort required to bring self-awareness from its original state, as a dimly glowing potential, to the incandescence of full realization. The two views do not really disagree, for the first concerns a state of which the waking self is unconscious, while the second is concerned with the means by which this 'unconscious' potentiality is integrated within the self-awareness of the fully evolved being.

When one reads the religious, mystical and philosophical literature of the world, one finds in almost every tradition that the stages of the path are classified and tabulated. But the classifications of one tradition seldom correspond exactly with those of another, for they are impositions of the mind on a spectrum of infinite gradations. Therefore, while it is useful and, indeed, necessary for us to understand that there is order in the levels of being, and that in some sense our growth can be measured against a schematic framework, it is futile to keep measuring one's progress against such scales. The scales are there as guides to understanding, not as marks of ego-achievement.

In much the same way that the inner work can, for convenience, be divided into two parts, (namely, work on the personal nature, on the one hand, and direct effort to reach the source of being, on the other), so dreams can be divided into two sorts—psychological dreams concerned with inhibitions and traumas, and throwing light on the first part of the work, and inspirational, 'Big' or mystical dreams which deal directly with the spiritual part of the work.

Thus, when *The Voice of the Silence*[1] says: 'Before the Soul can see, the Harmony within must be attained and fleshly eyes be rendered blind to all illusions', it sounds so logically true. In fact, however, it is an ideal statement, a general truth which is subject to many variations in practice. So, while it is generally true to say that before numinous or 'Big' dreams

[1] H.P. Blavatsky; Theosophical Publishing House, 1992.

will come, the dreamer must work his way through the cobwebbed dungeons of his subconscious mind, this need not always be the case. Sometimes it happens that a seeker is granted a vision of the light early in the work, as if to inspire him to face the darkness through which he must later grope his way.

Throughout, I am using the word 'dream' to signify any non-ordinary avenue of perception. The justification for doing this is that, the symbolic language of the psyche being much the same in all avenues, the method of interpretation is the same. This does not deny that such states may differ from one another, nor, possibly, that the visionary content natural to each state may have affinities for corresponding areas of our beings. For example, I have reason to suspect that hypnogogic visions—visions which can be watched while one is in a state half-way between waking and sleeping— have a particular affinity with the subtle physical or etheric level. But this need not imply that the meaning of the visions concerns the etheric. Nor is one man's experience of such correspondence proof that it is true for everyone.

Even within the standard definition of dreaming, there are more levels of perception than those in which there are or are not the rapid eye movements (REM) in the dreamer's body which modern research into the dream state associates with dreaming. However, it is not my concern here to distinguish and classify these different sorts of vision. I am concerned with the interpretation of visionary or auditory experiences outside those of the ordinary waking state.

What is this seeing without eyes and hearing without ears? Are we ascribing mystical significance to phenomena that can be explained by material events? It is not too difficult to imagine that a brain, well-stocked with memories from waking experience, could have its optic centre stimulated to produce images, as happens in fantasy and in many sorts of dreaming, both natural and drug induced. The difficulty comes in the case of visions that imply the existence of a power of seeing which is independent of the physical organs of sight, but is yet capable of seeing physical objects and scenes which have not previously been experienced by the seer's waking mind. Subtle organs of sight, distinct from the physical, are supposed by occultists to be part of the subtle body; and they suppose that the evolution of physical forms has always been preceded by and influenced by evolution on the subtle level. Be this as it may, it is one of the respectable views held by evolutionists that the specific nature of the human eye and its complex of optic nerve and visual cortex requires that the concept of the total system by which seeing is achieved had to pre-exist the evolution of its parts. It could not have happened by chance.

When dealing with this subject, one is constantly running up against problems of this sort to which we have, as yet, no convincing answer. However, if the fact is accepted, without explanation being demanded, one eventually finds one's acceptance honoured by events. In short, seeing of the sort in which the gross physical organs are not involved is found to be a simple fact of the inner worlds. Too great an emphasis laid on the demand for explanations, such that the questioner effectively refuses to step forward until his questions are answered, is apt to put him in the position of the man in the Buddha's story who, wounded by an arrow, refuses to have the arrow removed until he is told everything about the man who shot it, the make of the bow, and everything else. 'That foolish man will die,' said the Buddha, 'before he gets the answers to all his questions.'

In another context, I emphasize the importance of asking questions. In the first case (typified by the man in the Buddha's story in the previous paragraph), the questions stem from an ego-centred demand for answers to be given before the person agrees to move. In the other case (see the chapter on 'Big Dreams'), a mystery is shown in symbols, and if the right questions are not asked the person will not be able to move.

3

Seven Principles of Interpretation

The first and most important principle of dream analysis can best be put as a question: What is it in myself that is being represented by the content of the dream?

Dreams can tell us about other people and about events, but until this first question has been applied, the dream symbols and their meaning understood and found to be totally inapplicable to ourselves, we should not even think of applying them to others. We have no right to suppose that our psyches are concerned to tell us about other people before we have cleaned our own beings and made our minds free from prejudice, opinionatedness, self-righteousness, and the biases of most social, moral and religious teaching and conditioning. The converse is not true. If we find that our dreams are really telling us about other people, it does not imply that we have completed the task of personal purification. It may mean only that our worldly attitudes have invaded even our dreams. More often, we are being shown our own characteristics as we see them in the characters of others. Indeed, the projection of our own negative qualities onto others commonly precedes the introspection which leads to self-criticism.

If this lesson has not first been learned in waking life, we shall never succeed in understanding our dreams. The lesson is to put our own house in order before we attempt to put another's house in order, to criticize ourselves before we criticize others, to admire others but never to admire ourselves, and, most importantly, to understand that another person's irritating behaviour irritates us because we ourselves have the same or similar negative qualities.

The second principle is that our higher being urges us to growth, maturity and wholeness. It is the Spirit itself which sets us on the path to Self-discovery. Since our interpretations of the symbols of dream will inevitably be biased by our attitude towards them, we shall not be able to truly understand dreams or to distinguish between true and false dreams unless in our waking selves we fully accept the challenges of growth, and we desire to dedicate our lives to the service of the Spirit and to strive towards the wholeness that the Spirit itself seeks. To this end, it is therefore necessary to study sufficiently by reading, discussion and thought, to provide ourselves with a view of life which adequately encompasses our arising and the goal towards which we feel ourselves directed. If our life aims are greedy and selfish, we cannot expect help from that which is neither greedy nor selfish. In this context, therefore, we are not concerned with a view of dreams as aids, merely, to psychological adaptation to daily life and human relationships. Necessary though these are, they are but a part of the total work.

The third principle is that we must be prepared to face criticism. Most dreams are critical of us in the sense that they show us aspects of our lives that we do not like to look at. If we cannot accept criticism of ourselves in waking life, it will be difficult even to remember many dreams, let alone interpret them. When an interpretation reveals criticism, we must recognize that it is we who are criticizing ourselves. The interpreter may even be unaware that we find his interpretation painfully critical.

There are uncritical dreams, informatory dreams, and even reassuring and congratulatory dreams. But the basis of this principle of criticality in dreams is that, in general, our good qualities can be left to look after themselves. The less attention we pay to them, the less likely we shall be to spoil them by attaching self-pride to them. It is our bad qualities that need drawing to our attention, and particularly those qualities on which we pride ourselves but which are negative in relation to the Spirit, such as pride in social status, or in wealth. The desire to be constantly reassured and patted on the back is a bad quality because it derives from a sense of insecurity or inadequacy. If we have already congratulated ourselves, our dreams will have no reason to congratulate us further. And if we habitually praise ourselves, our dreams may turn sarcastic.

The fourth principle is that we must be prepared to descend into the lowest and dirtiest regions of ourselves. The Spirit's urge to wholeness demands that nothing shall remain outside its totality. Our minds must, therefore, be free to move at will throughout the psychic houses in which we dwell, from their cellars, drains and cesspools, through the dwelling rooms, bedrooms, bathrooms and lavatories, into cupboards, under and behind furniture, and into attics and lumber rooms. We cannot call our houses our own until there is nothing hidden, nothing that we fear or are ashamed to admit as ours. The Spirit encompasses everything, from its own numinous calm to tumultuous action, from high seriousness to dirty jokes, from celibate asceticism to passionate expressions of sexuality.

It should be obvious that if we cannot accept this principle with our waking minds, our waking minds will never be free to interpret dreams which open up unacceptable areas of our beings. We cannot clean the drains if we refuse to admit the existence of drains. We cannot understand the need to clean our vessels if we refuse to admit that our vessels are dirty. And we can clean nothing if we fear to change our ways of thinking, fear to challenge our inherited value systems, and fear to act in consonance with our new perceptions.

The fifth principle is the need to recognize that the power by which we dream is not merely the energy of repressed psychic material pushing up to consciousness. Of the presence of such repressed energies and of the sense of well-being that usually follows their release there can be no doubt. But the purpose in releasing them is not limited to achieving that sense of well-being and its consequent benefits in daily life. Unreleased, they act as blocks to our perception of higher states of consciousness. When they are released, we increasingly find that the content of dream and vision, instead of being confined to reflected images of repressed or unaccepted psychic material, shows us other aspects of objective being.

The cleaning of psychic content also cleans the windows of the soul. At first those windows appear only as reflecting surfaces in which we see images of our darker qualities. As we clean them, they become transparent membranes which reveal subtle worlds to our subtle vision whose reality is at least as great as that of the physical world we see through our physical organs of sense. Thus, the mirror of dream becomes the window of vision.

The sixth principle is the recognition that our dreaming is guided by an intelligence greater and wiser than that of our ordinary waking state, an intelligence that appears to be withdrawn and unconcerned with us and our affairs until we show ourselves ready to accept its guidance. Such acceptance has to be marked by our giving attention to dreams when they come, by our taking practical steps to remember and record them, and, most importantly, by our acting on what we understand. In other words, we have to treat the source of our dreams with as much respect as we would a respected living person to whom we had repaired for advice. While we might hope that such a person would not reject us at our first failure to follow his advice, we could hardly complain of rejection if, instead of trying to act on it, we merely wrote it down and did nothing about it. Such behaviour would be like that of people who get so much relief from unburdening their problems before a friend or teacher, and so much enjoy the attention it gets them, that they never trouble themselves to follow the advice given and so never free themselves of the causes. Tensions therefore mount again, and again they unburden themselves.

It must be emphasized that dreams are an aid to the inner inquiry, not a substitute for active inquiry. They may suggest an area of work and help us to understand it, but we have to take the suggestion and pursue it further. This is not a degraded educational system in which a student's work consists only of copying into his notebook what the teacher writes on the blackboard. We are research students, each doing original research with himself as the subject. Our teacher guides us, and we can refer to the accumulated sum of general knowledge existing in the world; but whether we have worked or merely copied will be judged by the results which will show as changes in ourselves.

The attitude to advice given in dream is, therefore, very different from surrender of personal responsibility or 'surrender to the unconscious'. Dreams never give us orders, for the simple reason that if we interpret a dream message as an order, it is ourselves who have interpreted it, or accepted an interpretation of it, as being an order. We are not being ordered; we are telling ourselves that we are being ordered. In fact, commands compel us to obey only in areas of our mechanicality. Any voices that order us in dream are, therefore, likely to represent not our higher selves, but our instincts or desires. Such a dream would not be ordering us, but drawing our attention to an area of thought or behaviour in which we are responding with mechanical obedience to the promptings of desire.

It can be made a seventh principle that everyone dreams. While many people may not want to concern themselves with dreams, no one can excuse himself from taking their advice simply on the grounds that he does not dream. Everybody dreams, some more, some less, but there are no exceptions. Whether we remember it or not, we dream. This fact has been confirmed by research which shows that brain activity corresponding to dream normally occurs at roughly ninety-minute intervals throughout the sleeping period.

The biggest factor in remembering dreams is attention. If dreams are not being remembered, attention is not being paid, and we have to assume that behind lack of attention is lack of will. In other words, people fail to remember their dreams because they do not want to remember them.

For most people, the only effort required to overcome a habitual disregard of dreams is a demonstration of willingness to record them. This can be done by placing a pencil and notebook or tape recorder beside the bed, together with a source of light. Before sleeping, the mind should be set with the determination (*samkalpa*) to write down or record the dream immediately on waking, in the same way that the mind can be set to awaken one at a particular time.

It is important to arouse oneself to the effort to record the dream as soon as one wakes. One has to refuse the temptation to lie comfortably, remembering the dream and excusing oneself from stirring on the grounds either that the dream is so clear one will never forget it, or that the memory is so fragile that movement will lose it. One may fall asleep again and find that the clearest dream has vanished, while the most fragile dream may often be recovered in the process of writing—one 'catches it by the tail' and pulls it out, bit by bit. Nor is there any justification for ignoring dim dreams and recording only brightly coloured, intense dreams. All may be equally significant for the work.

When one shares a room with others, it is advisable (and considerate to the others) to arrange a small source of light for writing. The glare from an overhead room light may drive all memory of a dream away, and one's reluctance to risk disturbing others can become another excuse for not making the effort to record; similarly with the reluctance to speak into a tape recorder in the presence of others.

It is advisable to record dreams in a notebook kept for the purpose, and to note the dates. Dreams often come in an ordered sequence, and references may be made to previous dreams; for this reason, jotting dreams down on loose scraps of paper is undesirable. Furthermore, we cannot expect to be able to understand all our dreams immediately, so it is necessary to go back over old material regularly, often understanding it only in the light of the fresh.

The normal discipline of the inner work is conducive to dream recall. I refer particularly to refusing comfort as an overriding consideration in sleeping conditions. One should not have too soft a bed, nor have more covering than is absolutely necessary in relation to local temperatures. In a hot climate, minimal use of cooling appliances can similarly be utilized to produce the light sleep conducive to dream recall. A pillow, if used, should be hard. Sleeping soon after the last meal at night should be avoided; if unavoidable, the meal should be light. A period of meditation should always precede sleep, and if it is desired to read, the subject matter of the book should be directly related to the spiritual path. Discursive thought should be stopped, and fantasy in particular should be avoided because the latter, even more than the former, burns up the store of psychic energy on which the inner effort is built.

When one finds that 'dreams are not coming'—a common periodical complaint—it is wise to look back over past material to see whether one has really made sufficient effort to understand and implement earlier messages. When dreams come regularly, it is easy to fall into the habit of expecting one's daily quota without doing any work for it. The inner guide may refuse to feed one with more until what has been given is digested, assimilated and made one's own. This is at least as frequent a cause of not getting dreams as is the inhibition of memory by the fear of unwelcome material. In the latter case, re-examination of recent material will often give the clue to the mental or psychic block.

It is usually good only to record—without analysis— dreams on waking. Attempts to interpret at the same time are apt to inhibit the process of recall, particularly when the dream may have an unwelcome meaning. If circumstances permit, interpretation should be taken up after one's early morning programme, but before starting the day's work. If this is not possible, as is often the case for women who have to see children off to school and husbands off to work, it is advisable at least to read through the night's dream material before getting lost in the day's routine. This may stimulate further memories which can be noted.

There is always time to think about dreams during the day, as there is always time to quieten the mind in meditation. People who say they have no time are actually filling their minds with continual and unnecessary chatter. They need to get their priorities sorted out.

Conditions suitable for dream interpretation vary widely between individuals. A person accustomed to introspection, self-analysis and self-criticism may not find it difficult to understand the criticism of and the challenges to his basic assumptions which constitute the messages of so many dreams. But a person who is not so accustomed, and whose self-confidence is based only on those very elements in his nature which are under attack, may find that his intelligence refuses to grapple with the symbols of the dream language. The more reluctant one is to accept criticism, the further removed are the dream symbols from direct reference to the subject criticized, and so the more difficult to connect. This is because awareness of unwelcome criticism inhibits the dream content from entering waking awareness; we 'forget' the dream. The message is, therefore, couched in symbols which at first appearance have nothing unwelcome about them.

It has to be remembered that while we may have little or no resistance to criticism of some parts of ourselves, we may cherish other parts so greatly that attacks on them seem to threaten our very existence and all that we hold dear. So much is this the case that even a person who normally finds little difficulty in interpreting his own dreams will find some dreams that he either cannot understand, or that yield no new insights when subjected to his customary analytical procedure.

For all people some of the time, and for some people all of the time, another person is needed to assist in the process of interpretation. Sometimes this has to be a person of greater experience, sometimes it is enough that the helper is able to see the dreamer's problem, either because he has previously dealt with it, or because he happens not to be inhibited in this particular area—it is always easier to see through the other man's inhibitions—and often it is enough that the helper acts only as a 'sounding board' to whom the dreamer can talk out his thoughts about his dreams and get an intelligent response which stimulates his own understanding. Whoever this person may be, it must be someone to whom one can entrust one's deepest and most personal secrets. If one fears to have one's confidences betrayed, both dreaming and interpretation will be inhibited.

Many people find it helpful to note down their thoughts and associated ideas about their dreams, finding that the process of noting prevents the loss of insights and stimulates new ones. In any case, such interpretations as are arrived at should be written down, preferably in the same notebook in which the dream is recorded.

The inner intelligence provides a message in dream, throwing light upon one of our problems or distorted views of reality. It proceeds to expand upon that problem, leading us through its ramifications into other and related matters, gradually creating an area of order within the chaos. Not all messages are understood at their first presentation, and problems are seldom solved at the first attempt. Dreams, therefore, tend to present the same problem in different modes, perhaps over a period of weeks, until one of them is understood. If we then look back at the earlier, unsolved dreams, we see that they were saying the same thing in different ways. But the moment the meaning of the series is grasped, we find the subject matter changes. A fresh problem or a fresh aspect of the old one is being presented. But it has to be noted that if the subject matter does not change after we think we have found an interpretation, then it is probably not the right interpretation.

Sometimes, the subject matter changes even when not understood. It is as if the teacher said: 'Leave it. We will come back to it later.' But we find ourselves taken back to problems we thought solved. The process can be likened to the movement of a gramophone needle over the surface of a disc. If we imagine that the quadrants of the circle are allocated to different subjects, then each subject is repeated with each revolution of the disc. But with each revolution the needle creeps nearer to the centre, as work under the guidance of dreams leads us towards the centre of our being.

The manner in which dream interpretation helps us is not limited to the messages themselves and the guidance they provide to the inner work. In order to understand the language of dream we are compelled to adapt our minds to a new way of thinking, freeing them from the rigid coordinates of the standard educational systems and from the inhibiting influences of our social upbringing.

The ordered sequence in which a subject is unfolded through a series of dreams is liable to be interrupted by dreams that throw light on one's reactions to day-to-day events. A disturbing event may be commented upon immediately. If this is not understood, one may find an interpreter unsuccessfully trying to bend a dream into the shape required to fit the current series, when it is really concerned with an entirely separate incident. One has to be alert to catch such changes when they come.

Trial and error is normal to the process of dream interpretation, an erroneous interpretation often stimulating the dreamer to produce the extra evidence needed to unravel the plot. However, it is not always easy to distinguish between a genuine rebuttal of an attempted interpretation, and what Freudians call 'resistance'. Intuition, therefore, plays a considerable part in the way an interpreter handles a dreamer. While a false interpretation must not be forced upon a dreamer, the mere fact of non-acceptance is not proof that the interpretation is false. Nonetheless, Jung is right in saying that an interpreter should not be satisfied with the correctness of his reading unless it satisfies the dreamer.

This problem is particularly difficult for someone interpreting his own dreams, for it calls for unusual honesty and humility to admit to an unflattering estimation of one's own character or to accept an interpretation which challenges one's basic assumptions. Often, however, an interpretation may be close to the mark, but just sufficiently distant for the dreamer truthfully, though not altogether honestly, to reject it. Honesty demands that a close miss be admitted for what it is, namely, something that reveals the mark.

An interpreter's job is to help the dreamer arrive at an interpretation which is acceptable to him, and which is meaningful because it throws light on aspects of his nature. It is not his job to show off his versatility or to force his own opinions on the dreamer. He has to be particularly careful not to get his own problems mixed with the dreamer's, and so give an interpretation which applies to himself but not to the dreamer. It is to guard against such dangers that psychological schools usually insist that an analyst first be analysed himself, but this seldom entirely avoids the difficulty. A better safeguard seems to lie in the dreamer rapidly learning enough about interpretation and about his own nature to be able to protect himself and, perhaps, to help the analyst in his turn. However, when working with beginners it usually falls to the interpreter to do most of the work and to provide an interpretation, but if students are not encouraged to do their own work, they will never learn.

Another danger to be avoided is the common assumption that the dream must be dealing with the problem uppermost in the dreamer's mind. This may sometimes be the case, but to assume it always to be so leads to gross distortions. I have frequently had to listen to people talking with considerable insight on some matter that was really upsetting them, on the basis of a dream that had nothing to do with it. However, it often happens that discussion arising out of a dream is valuable to all concerned, even though at the end of it all the dream itself remains unsolved.

Perhaps the best way to treat such a question is to regard it as one key out of the many which might unlock the dream. Try it and see if it fits. If it does not, then try another. Another key in the same category is recent events. Many dreams show us our inadequacies in immediate relationships, and they use as pointers those moments when we have behaved stupidly or have bottled up our anger or hurt without then opening the bottle and distilling its unpleasant contents. In such matters, our dreams may give us a reaction the same night, perhaps interrupting a sequence that was unfolding day by day. Such dreams are particularly difficult to understand at a later date because the references have been forgotten.

Some interpreters, having found a formula which makes sense of many of their clients' dreams, then make the mistake of using it to the exclusion of everything else; e.g., it is all either Freudian sex, Jungian archetypes or Melanie Klein and her good and bad breasts. This is the sort of thing that has given rise to the saying that there are as many interpretations as there are analysts. In practice, most analysts will be able to say something about a particular dream which the dreamer will find meaningful and useful, but this need not imply that the dream has been interpreted. I personally prefer the view that each dream has only one correct interpretation, even though I often find myself compelled to give alternative readings and leave the dreamer to choose the best fit.

One therefore needs a bunch of keys—Freudian, Jungian, childhood's traumas, anxiety, the sense of inadequacy, etc.— which one tries out on one's dreams, selecting the one that fits the best and throws most light on one's inner state. Eventually one learns to let each dream speak for itself.

Another danger to watch out for is the way some dreamers, as they rise from dream to the waking state, take control of the dream and cause it to have a happy ending. An instinctive escape mechanism seems to be at work by which they seek to avoid the threat of hurtful criticism.

4

The Language of Dreams

The great problem with dreams is that they have to be interpreted. But the word 'interpretation' must never be taken as an attempt to bring the source of dreams under the control of our egotistic attitudes.

Dreams speak to us in their own language, so our task is really to translate that language into terms that we can comprehend, and to do it with as little distortion as possible.

We therefore have to learn a new language, or to relearn a very ancient one. It is the universal language of the soul, the language of feeling: signs, symbols, the primal language of our racial childhood, pictographic ideograms from which language derives, basic to man as man.

By virtue of this fact, it is not really a difficult language to learn, once one has found someone who knows it. Like all living languages, however, it has a number of dialects, each with its own vocabulary. The commonest dialects, and the ones easiest to learn, are those spoken by the different psychological schools. It is useful and even necessary to know them, but one has to avoid adopting their accents. For example, while we must be free to borrow from Freud's insights into the interpretation of dream symbols, we must not put ourselves into a position where every dream is interpreted with a Freudian accent.

The way to avoid this problem is to be clear about one's aim. Even though a lot of the work we shall have to do will be the same as regular psychological analysis in which the analyst's aim would be to make us well-adapted citizens, we, by contrast, aim to use the psychological tools to free ourselves from the compulsions of desire, so that we can pass beyond the surface of the waking mind and find whatever it is that is there. To this end, therefore, it is helpful to familiarize ourselves with the mystical teachings of the world. In spite of its being second-hand information of limited value, we shall benefit from the way the real truths resonate with their symbols.

This question of clarity of purpose is of vital importance, for although some knowledge of the dream language—with its punning, its substitutions of persons, and associative thinking—is necessary, and although we ought to be familiar with some theories concerning the structure of the psyche, with its inhibitions and complexes, if we are to go further than the psychological schools, we must also have a clear idea of the goal towards which the inquiry is directed and have a knowledge of what is required of those who aim for that goal.

Indeed, we are caught in a curious contradiction. While it must constantly be reiterated that we do not know whether there is anything to be found until we find it, it is necessary to cultivate a feeling for the sorts of messages the psyche is likely to give us. This calls for extreme honesty, for it is only too easy to persuade ourselves that dreams are giving us messages consonant with our personal views, when in fact they may be challenging or correcting them. This is one of the reasons why it is advisable to find a guide who is familiar with the road.

If we already know what dreams may say, then what need have we of attending to them? And if dreams tell us what we do not know, then how can we be sure of their truth?

On the level of psychological interpretation, the answer is relatively simple: we may be familiar with psychological theory, but lack the insight needed to apply it to ourselves. When dreams give us insight into the workings of our natures, we interpret by referring to theory. When the two meet and agree, it results in our obtaining actual, as opposed to theoretical, understanding. However, if we have no theoretical knowledge, then the problem of interpretation becomes more difficult. There are other systems of thought and symbolism by which understanding can be reached, but in that case we must be familiar with those ideas and symbols. If we are not, then the communication gap becomes too great to be bridged. We are then faced with the need to build our own system of thought, without the aid of work previously done by others.

Much the same thing applies to the analysis of dreams relating to aspects of being of which we have had no previous experience; this being quite different from the psychology of remembered or forgotten life experiences. If the message of a dream were to be too different from anything with which we were familiar, we would have no means of relating it to any known framework or body of knowledge and so have no means of understanding it. In other words, we have to be close to the next step in understanding before we can be shown it. And even then it takes an effort to distinguish the unfamiliar in it from the necessarily familiar terms in which it is described. We, therefore, have to know something about what we are seeking before we become capable of recognizing it when we find it.

Anyone can experience higher states of being, but if those states cannot be related to the here and now, they cannot be integrated within the normal awareness of this world, and the cognitive aspect of such experience will be lost. The Seer may affirm the wondrous reality of the Spirit, but he may not understand how it relates to everyday life. This may bear on the transcendental philosophies which deny significance of any sort to the so-called 'lower' levels of existence and it does account for the phenomenon of the 'simple saint' and for many of the contradictions in behaviour which are found in men of partial attainment.

This, then, is the reason for study, discussion and thought about the Spirit, about the nature of being, about man, and about ourselves. Even though we know that such head-learning cannot substitute for experience, we must also know that without some framework of reference not even the ultimate experience would convey its full import to us, especially when it appears in a form totally different from what we might have expected.

Therefore, besides reading books on psychology and dream analysis, one should make oneself conversant with the mythologies and philosophies of the world, so that one can get the most out of dreams. For, by familiarizing oneself with mythological material, one provides the psyche with a wealth of images in its own language which it can then draw on to convey its messages. The study of other systems of visual symbolism, such as the Tarot and astrology, is also useful for providing the psyche with a vocabulary with which both it and the waking mind are familiar. The psyche naturally tends to draw upon images with which we are familiar, as any teacher will try to use words the pupil understands, and so it uses the figures of people and events in the local environment.

However, it is both a part of the inner work and an intention of the psyche that we should open our minds to the universality of the Spirit by seeing its expressions everywhere, and not remain limited to the parochial outlook of our home culture.

We are all familiar with the fact that dreams convey their messages in symbols, but we are apt to forget that speech and writing are also symbolic. These marks on the paper before you are symbols of sounds, and the sounds are symbols of ideas or mental content. There are perhaps as many written or spoken symbols for a tree as there are human languages, and anyone seeing a tree will name it as such in his language. What we must understand in this case is that our mental image of a tree is a symbolic interpretation of sense stimuli: it is a symbol of the tree. What, then, is a tree? In so far as a tree has real being, it is an expression of the forces of life and consciousness which built it; it symbolizes those forces. Thus, there is nothing strange in the fact that dreams speak in symbols.

As we have said, the symbols of dream are a sort of primal language, the universal language of the soul. They are not primitive or inarticulate. They convey ideas as profound, exact, detailed, abstract or practically applicable as can the sounds and signs of any language.

But there are also dream references to persons and events which are relatively private to each dreamer, private in the sense that an interpreter cannot be expected to know that a dream character is the dreamer's uncle or know the dreamer's personal associations with a particular colour. What he can know, however, is that if the colour of a particular object yields nothing in the context of basic colour symbolism, but is vivid enough for the dreamer to have remarked it, then it is almost certain that that colour is associated strongly with some particular memory private to the dreamer.

The difficulty in grasping the meaning of a dream image often lies in the number of different levels on which it can be interpreted. In the great Indian epic, the Mahabharata, Sri Krishna explains how his behaviour is always appropriate to his sphere of actions. 'When I am in the world of the gods,' he says, 'I behave as a god. In the world of the *gandharvas* (angelic beings) I behave as a *gandharva*. And in the world of men, I behave as a man.' Similarly with the images of dream, their interpretation has to be appropriate to the level on which the dreamer is functioning.

It is usually, though not always, the case that for a long time we may be faced with dreams which must be interpreted in relation to the lowest levels. This is so both because the work must be based on firm foundations, and because the full implications of the higher levels of interpretation will not be grasped if their relationship to the lower is not accepted. Take, for instance, the phallic stone which is Shiva's representation in the temples of India. If its phallic connotations are considered obscene, then it will be impossible for the seeker to accept that the procreative power is not being used merely as a primitive and crude parallel of the divine creativity, but that the microcosmic power is the same as the macrocosmic. Consequently, he will not appreciate the need to free his view of the human phallus from his early hygiene training which negatively associated it with its excretory function, perhaps with dirt and perhaps with moral guilt.

As a general principle, it can be taken that the meaning of a dream image is what it means to the dreamer. This is not an exclusive principle, because the key to a dream often lies in the hands of the person to whom it is taken for interpretation. When the latter is the case, it is a demonstration that the range of consciousness is not restricted to the contents of our individualized minds—minds whose content we like to think of as being private to ourselves.

It is also generally true that the lower the level to which the dream refers, the more its interpretation will depend on the dreamer's personal associations with the images.

Associative thinking is, as it were, part of the structure of the dream language. Without letting the mind run away entirely, it has to be allowed to play around the dream image so that associated images arise. Not every image will be relevant. Intuition plays an important role in the process of selecting those images which are appropriate to the dreamer's immediate need. The dreamer's own associations take priority over the interpreter's. However, since all men are very similar to each other, the run of association will regularly lead other people to the same or a similar conclusion as the dreamer's. This is what makes it possible for one person to interpret another's dream.

It seldom happens that a dream can be interpreted entirely without the dreamer's associations and the information he can give about figures in the dream. The key to the meaning may be in the name of a dream person (e.g., *Nirmala*: clean, without dirt, or Thomas, with the association of 'doubting Thomas'), the dreamer's assessment of his character (e.g., a lazy fellow), in relationship (e.g., 'vaguely related' = something connected with the subject but not clearly seen, or 'a houseful of relations' = the general problem of family relationships), in the situation where they met (e.g., 'on holiday' = the dreamer's tendency to take a holiday from the work), or the dream figure reminding one of someone else (e.g., 'like my father').

Often it may seem that the collection of such associated data is compounding the confusion, but in truth the process is akin to that of translating a sentence in an unknown language with the help of a dictionary. Each word turned up in the dictionary has numerous possible meanings, any one of which could have been intended by the author. Similarly with dreams, one word may give the clue to the sense in which other words must be read, and sometimes the context of the sentence in the setting of the dream allows the interpreter to infer the manner in which it must be taken. There are also dreams whose images, translated into direct speech, make up a simple sentence: e.g., 'I was meeting people, but I could not see them clearly because my shadow was falling on them.' The 'shadow' is the psychological term for a person's negative qualities which he tends to see reflected in others but fails to see in himself, and so does not see them clearly for what they are in themselves.

It is very important to keep a flexible attitude towards dream symbols. No attempt should be made to make a dictionary of fixed meanings; no matter how frequently a symbol is found to have the same meaning, other dreamers or the same dreamer on other occasions will use the same image with a different meaning. Even a common equation, such as that animals refer to the instinctive life, needs cautious handling. The instinctive dog of the Western dreamer is replaced by the monkey in India, where a dog, particularly a black one, leads Indians to think of death. An example of instinctive feelings represented by an animal was the dream of an Indian woman whose daughter was getting married. She dreamed that a prehistoric animal was running off with the girl, showing her that her current anxieties arose from her primitive protective instinct and not because she was sensing negative qualities in the bridegroom. A camel makes many people think of grumbling, but it could also refer to 'the stars are setting and the caravan / starts for the dawn of nothing . . .' And 'the King of beasts', the almost universally accepted symbol of courage, sometimes yields his meaning in the not uncommon mispronunciation of his name in India: 'loins'.

Private associations often take precedence over the commonly accepted meanings of symbols. A tram would usually associate with a mental attitude or activity inflexibly running on fixed tracks, 'a one-track mind', or as in the limerick, 'a being that moves in determinate grooves / in fact, not a bus, but a tram.' But a woman who frequently dreamt that she was riding a tram did not find this a rewarding line of thought. She then remembered that as a young woman going to art school she regularly travelled on a tram. The associated feeling was that the tram, through its association with the art school, represented liberation from the restrictions imposed on her at home. For her, the tram represented freedom. Associative thinking is at the root of puns, which are common in dream and in many forms of joke, as in a dream which made a man laughingly admit that he thought his cock smaller than the one next door. Often, also, there is a play on words, as in a dream where a mother saw that her child was getting, not *scarletina* but *violetina*. Looking in the dictionary to see if there was any such word (always a useful gambit), nothing of that form was found under violet, but the preceding word was violent, which was the clue to the dream.

The psyche is cosmopolitan in its choice of images, seeming to be aware not only of what is in the dreamer's mind, but also of what he is capable of discovering in the future if he applies himself to hunting the sources of dream symbols. Frequently, the psyche draws indiscriminately from memories of the past, present and future, so that the dreamer may find himself startled into remembering a dream of the night before by his being confronted with an event whose details were in the dream, yet of which he could have had no previous knowledge. As a young man on my first morning in a new job, I found myself in entirely unfamiliar surroundings which precisely matched the dream situation I had been in on waking. Blurting out my astonishment, I found that my two new colleagues were both already interested in precognitive dreams and related subjects—a rare situation in the 1930s, and this led to a rewarding friendship. Such fortunate consequences do not always follow. It is fortunate enough to obtain personal experience of the fact of precognition, an experience that challenges conventional views of life and its purpose.

I have previously mentioned that the dream language has local or cultural dialects whose symbols may be those of the dreamer's culture, class, religion, etc. Similarly, although the language or dialect is basically the same, individuals tend to dream in an idiom that is as peculiar to themselves as is a man's speech pattern or habit of thought. One may come across several individuals who dream in the same idiom, but such similarity in idiom is not necessarily related to their sharing a common culture or a common speech.

One of the problems in interpreting dreams, therefore, is that one has to familiarize oneself with the idiom of each person. A new associate's dreams may at first seem to yield no meaning until one obtains an intuitive grasp of his idiomatic mode of expression. It also happens on occasion that one is successfully reading the meaning of one person's dreams and is then required immediately to switch to the interpretation of another's. Although on previous occasions the second person's dreams presented no great difficulty, on this occasion the interpreter's mind seems to lack insight. The reason appears to be that the idiom of the two dreamers differs. Having adjusted his mind to the idiom of the first, the interpreter has difficulty in making an immediate adjustment to the idiom of the second. It is, therefore, advisable to allow an interval between the interpretation of different people's dreams. For the same reason, I personally find it better not to handle the dreams of both a husband and his wife in the same session, even though it is often helpful to have both present.

Under the general heading of 'idiom', I include such idiosyncrasies as the patterns in which dreams occur. For instance, one man may habitually have one long and involved dream in which one event runs into the next, yet each event may in fact refer to a quite different matter, while another may have a series of separate dreams, all referring to the same matter. In the former case, if one interpretation was to be sought that would satisfy every event in the dream, it would result in frustration. On the other hand, the interpreter must be sure that the results justify such separate treatment of the parts of a dream and not use this as a device to gloss over his failure to perceive a consistent theme running through the whole.

5

The Imprinted Mind: Social Conditioning

At the end of Chapter 1 we said: '. . . the first images to rise into dream from the threshold of consciousness are felt to be so frightening or so disgusting that the person either forgets the dream or is too ashamed to relate it. The most common subject of such dreams is sex, and that is why so much attention has to be given to it in the following pages.'

The events of our infancy and formative years strongly influence both our choice of interests and our attitudes towards sex. The latter tends to determine the degree of ease or difficulty we have in checking our adult sexual interest and associated outflows in order to build up sufficient libidinous potential to help us on our path. Therefore, if the first reason for the descent into the murk of the subconscious mind is the need to accept everything within us, the second reason is that we have to free the erotic flow from the outgoing channels into which it has been diverted by the environmental and ideological conditioning of the cultures in which we have grown up.

In later life, many of these matters appear as disturbing factors in the attempt to control the mind, making the task so difficult that it brings many people to despair. Our thoughts seem to develop a life of their own and drag us off as captives. However, this in itself gives us a clue to the nature of the problem: it is not so much the thoughts themselves that we have to control, as the inarticulate powers of desire and fear which drive them. Thoughts or mental images can thus be seen as indicators by which we recognize the libidinous flows which give thoughts their seeming autonomy.

Since an examination of the libido lies in the field of regular psychoanalysis, we can use psychological methods to great advantage, provided we never lose sight of our inner aim. For example, if we find our minds (and dreams) driven by sexual inhibitions, our intention of freeing ourselves from such inhibitions is not in order to enjoy uninhibited sexual relations but, firstly, to free our minds from the limitations imposed by inhibitions and, secondly, to free the psychic energy imprisoned by inhibitions for application to the inner work. If certain thoughts and behaviour patterns are seen to be connected with a deep-seated insecurity, we do not aim to build a more integrated personality which will lead to greater success in life and therefore to enhanced self-confidence. We seek, rather, security in identification with that which is unshaken by any worldly threats because it is neither body, nor personality, nor anything the world can touch.

Dreams support such views, though they never thrust them upon us; we see the references only if our eyes are open to them. Every dreamer has dreams suited to his state. However, since this is not a general study of dreams but is confined to the dreaming of people on the inner path, I do not aim to cover the dreams of people who have no aim in life other than the various modes of personal ambition or attaining a stable, well-adjusted personality. Nonetheless, it remains a fact that much of the ground covered is the same for all, often if not always starting with those distortions of outlook imposed on all of us by reason of our humanity.

We are born into animal bodies with animal instincts and desires. In our early years, our animal components preponderate, and it is usually not until we have become physically mature that, if we are fortunate, we wake up to the necessity of working on the task of becoming fully human. In infancy and throughout our youth we are subjected in varying degrees to massive behavioural and social conditioning through which we are trained to behave as if we were human—as human as the level of society into which we have been born.

Much of this conditioning is essential to the survival of human society and is therefore unavoidable. Methods vary but slightly between different cultures, each culture being convinced that its methods are the best. In contemporary 'developed' societies many experiments have been made in infant training, often in reaction against the seeming harshness of traditional disciplinary methods. The results vary from being mildly beneficial to the people affected, to producing monstrous caricatures who, never having been disciplined when young, grow up to revolt against what they perceive to be stultifying middle-class social restrictions and capitalist values. Conversely, societies divorced from their instinctual roots are producing increasing numbers of children whose ignorant parents treat them with such brutality that they either refuse involvement in an inhuman world and withdraw into an autistic state of dream and fantasy, or become psychological cripples, unable to escape the traumas of their upbringing, taking their revenge upon the world.

One could argue that an infant is to some extent like a little animal, brought into a human household, which is taught to please its owners by a system of rewards and punishments. At first, its own awareness is centred on the basic processes of living creatures, eating and excreting, associated with the psychic experiences of comfort and discomfort, pleasure and pain. Superimposed on this instinctual little animal is a human awareness, a person, usually dependent on parental love and attention to assure it that, in spite of birth traumas and the discomforts that reach it through its new body, life may not be such a bad thing after all.

This duality is what makes infancy such a highly sensitive period. The social necessity of training young children to behave at least as well as other children of their group is apt to conflict with the psychic needs or expectations of the incoming soul (or focus of consciousness). This problem is exacerbated by the human child's long period of helplessness when it can neither fend for itself nor think for itself. Its instinctive responses are not as developed as those of any other young animal, nor are its mother's. A human mother has to be taught how to look after a child; and perhaps it is due to women having retained some of the maternal instinct and to a certain resilience in human infants that the race survives. It is hard to believe that the teaching given to mothers is responsible.

Every human society has rules which separate the two functions of taking in food and voiding the residue. In some primitive forms of life, the same orifice is used for both functions, but in all the higher forms they have been separated physically, and in most of them the separation has become built into their instinctual behaviour patterns. In humans, the replacement of instinctual behaviour in this respect by consciously imposed hygienic standards appears to be a late development.

In many peasant societies, mothers feed their children whenever they show signs of being hungry, and not much fuss is made over a child's uncontrolled excretions. But in the 'developed' areas of society, the establishment of regular eating habits and hygiene training are begun early because, both in the mother's interests and in the interests of society, it is more convenient to have a child that cries for food at regular times and that makes messes only in the proper places, than to have hungry wails at all hours and a baby that has learned to enjoy wallowing in its own waste.

During hygiene training, the mother shows pleasure when the baby learns to use the toilet, and displeasure, supported by grimaces, sounds of disgust, and words such as 'bad', 'naughty', 'dirty', when it soils itself. How much the mother feels the disgust she shows depends on her own 'disgust threshold', which is determined partly by instinctive responses and partly by the sort of conditioning she herself received as an infant. The more she feels, the more the impact on the child, for children are sensitive to emotional states, even when not grossly expressed. Particularly in the early stages of infancy, the mother's pleasure is the child's reward and her displeasure its punishment.

As opposed to what a well-conditioned adult thinks to be a 'natural' disgust for excreta in all forms, a small child has no disgust about its own. As a child grows, it takes an interest in its own body, bodily functions, and the productions of its body. Left to itself, it touches and tastes its own excreta, a fascinating material which it believes itself to have created. Caught in such an activity, or even showing its interest, the child attracts displeasure and perhaps punishment.

The child's developing interests then turn towards the bodies of other children. It compares its own body and organs with theirs, and is often particularly interested in seeing another's anus and, if possible, the act of defecation, because it cannot see its own. The consequences of getting caught are again painful. Of course, many children are never allowed the opportunity to indulge such interests, some having their natural responses so repressed that they grow up to feel guilty even when such a thought enters the mind. There are perhaps less voyeurs than otherwise in societies where such interests are not repressed.

Where this sort of behaviour earns children parental disapproval, they quickly learn what sorts of group behaviour must be kept secret from the grown-ups. They develop a double standard, doing what they like with others of the same sort without inhibition, but concealing even their interests in the presence of adults. They indulge their interests but know that the grown-ups disapprove, and are, therefore, pursued by guilt. They continue to do it despite the grown-ups' disapproval, which means that they are what the grown-ups say they are: 'bad', 'wicked', 'dirty', etc. Since the grown-ups disapprove, evidently they never did such things or never had such interests. By the same token, the people who say the children are bad and wicked must themselves be good. Perhaps no child ever made this equation consciously, but this is, in effect, the conclusion the child comes to.

In societies where parental sex goes on in the presence of children, the child's reaction is different and not very healthy, but where parental sex is concealed, even young adults have a curiously ambiguous attitude towards their parents, knowing that they owe their births to their parents' sexual activities, yet being unable to accept their parents' capacity for erotic enjoyment.

Both eating and excreting have problems and traumas

associated with them, but excretion has more, partly because hygiene training begins there, and partly because the excretory functions are associated with the genital areas, so that attitudes formed towards excretion become associated with attitudes towards sex. No matter how enlightened later sexual instruction may be, these effects of pre-memory conditioning are deeply impressed and extremely difficult to eradicate.

The child cannot, and few adults do, understand the significance of these cultural practices, which have the effect of repressing children's interest in the genital area. The practical social necessity of hygiene training is linked to the equally practical necessity of preventing illicit sex and the consequence of too many unwanted children, and both are confused with dirt and moral wickedness. We are, therefore, faced with an unfortunate situation in which the laudable attempt to persuade 'little animals' to behave as human beings results in a large area of life—everything below the navel—being overshadowed by feelings of disgust and the concept of sin.

The problem has not been solved by the modern sexual revolution, which has been made possible by contraceptive technology combined with psychological insights into the mechanism of inhibition and the means for its removal. Freedom to enjoy uninhibited sex is no more a sign of a strictly human progress in the developed societies than it is in those tribal societies which seem to have always enjoyed it. The question is whether these insights help us to control the mind, help us to overcome the immensely powerful compulsions of the erotic energy and, if so, to what end. To what image of the human state are we referring when we speak of a 'strictly human progress'? To what sort of humanity is the 'little animal' expected to aspire? The answer will have something to do with the cultural achievements of mankind, the cultivation of the energies of life and intelligence which made those achievements possible, and all that these imply in terms of the development of an incandescent awareness in man which perceives the timeless significance of all that is unfolded in the field of time.

Though we need not dig into its historical roots, there is a worldwide tradition, almost as ancient as man, that the libidinous energies of sex can be canalized to flow in other directions of interest and achievement. Such achievements may be anything from courage in hunters and warriors, to skill in crafts, learning, intellectual acumen, magical powers and spiritual vision. In the present day, newspapers discuss the period of sexual abstinence to be observed by football teams before important matches. Traditional explanations of the modus operandi may be crude and superstitious, but the fact is real. Restraint of libidinous outflows causes a build-up of psychic potential which gets utilized in other fields of activity, sometimes compulsively, sometimes intentionally.

Sexual abstinence before the hunt has been practised by hunting tribes from time immemorial. At the beginnings of civilization, when the need to impose sexual restraints in the interests of human development was recognized, its imposition as a cultural practice tended to be achieved through superstitious beliefs, for the benefits of restraint are obtained whether or not one understands the mechanism. For example, what is called the rising of Kundalini is a fact, and it makes no difference whether one thinks of it in terms of psychic energy or in the illusory anatomical terms of Indian yoga. The benefits of restraint are particularly relevant in their application to children. If their awareness of genital sexuality can be postponed until puberty, and their erotic curiosity directed into other activities and studies, the channels of interest which have been opened will continue to flow in later life, in spite of their then enjoying the pleasure and release of the sexual outlet—an outlet that would otherwise be like the drain plug on a water tank, for so long as it is open, no pressure can be built.

If the application of this principle were intelligently understood, there might not be so many distorted psyches— victims sacrificed to the general development of mankind. For the blind imposition of restraint through unreasoning moral condemnation and superstitious fears inevitably leaves a great deal to chance, and chance produces statistical averages which result in as many failures as successes.

Unfortunately, no better way of handling the matter is known. But its effectiveness is demonstrated by the nations and sections of society which have adopted it, for they are invariably associated with the greatest achievements, even if the world as a whole is beginning to question the wisdom of canalizing the power into the traditional channels.

Left to chance and the vagaries of social organizations, the actual results of this cultural principle are chaotic. Parents who were themselves conditioned in childhood to believe sex to be dirty and sinful, and have imposed similar beliefs on their children, actually and rightly behave as if it were nothing of the sort. Consequently, there are many instances where children are exposed to adult behaviour which comes in conflict with both what the children have been taught to believe and with what adults believe children ought to be taught. Children in crowded slum conditions, fully aware of parental copulation, may be stimulated to incestuous relations long before puberty. Even in the economically advantaged classes, children may often be introduced to sex by servants, older children, and perverted adults. And it has to be remembered that none of this is 'unnatural'; in some tribal societies, children from the age of five or so are sent to sleep in the 'club' where they pair off and sleep together. Indeed, it is the control of sex and the sublimation of its energies which is, as the alchemists put it, 'against nature'.

The effects of unrestrained eroticism are subtle and, therefore, difficult to demonstrate in the present ambience of materialistic scientism, which ignores everything that cannot be observed by the sense organs. Even among psychologists there is a tendency to ascribe the psychic depletion of over-indulgence to a guilt complex. While not denying the effect of guilt in many cases, and while not denying that exceptionally gifted men sometimes arise in cultures which impose little or no sexual restraint, it is generally true that all human culture and all civilizations have been built on the restraint of sexual activity, and that where this restraint has weakened, there has been a corresponding deterioration in tribal, civic, and national achievement.

People who argue that this doctrine of sublimation is superstitious nonsense and that human achievements derive from some other set of conditions, appear to be in the curious condition of denying the ground they stand on, for they have all been subjected in childhood to the sort of conditioning which canalized their energies to the point where they can now frame such arguments.

In most cases, the conditioning was such that sex, however pleasurable or productive of little darlings, is almost unmentionably improper and 'dirty' and so cannot be admitted as being the source of the *Fifth Symphony*, Chartres cathedral or even of the British government—which all goes to show how warped the mind can get, for only the crudest explanations of the process of sublimation suppose a necessary awareness of the connection between the energies that are sublimated and excitation of the genitals. Indeed, the very basis of the principle in its application to children is that a child's awareness of genital excitation should be as little as possible until it is old enough to accept responsibility for restraining its own instinctive desires. 'When ignorance is bliss, 'tis folly to be wise.' The curiosity normal to a child will lead it to experiment with anything it is told about, especially when it is within so easy a reach as its own genitals. Parents long ago discovered that 'babies born under gooseberry bushes' were better for the child than the bare facts of life.

Protection against the wastefulness of early sexual experience is not the only advantage of ignorance in the young. Sexual fantasy can burn up as much psychic energy as can the act itself. Indeed it may waste more, for the reason that it uses up psychic energy directly, whereas the physical act may, in the case of a child, burn up little more than the physical energies of its play.

It, therefore, appears more important to restrain infantile genital awareness than to restrain adult sexuality. With the libidinous flows of the early years canalized into mental activity, energy will continue to be available to the mind even when adult sexuality develops. An 'upward flow' established in childhood will continue in some measure throughout life. But if genital satisfaction is achieved early, the upward flow into mentation is starved, the upward channels are not opened or enlarged, and then, when adult sexuality develops, it drains out all available potential.

This rather materialistic description is not to be taken literally. There is no crude anatomy, as supposed by some of the Indian yoga systems, which describe a tube running up the spine through which semen can be made to travel to the brain. We are concerned with subtle or psychic energies whose 'flow' is analogous to the 'flow' of interest. If interest is centred on genital satisfaction, the energy flows there. If it is centred on intellectual pursuits or on scientific research, the energy flows there. And if it is centred on spiritual growth, the energy becomes available for such growth.

6

Traumas

It is a fortunate person whose childhood contained no shocking or painful events which have distorted later responses in relationships or towards ordinary life situations. The effects of such events are described as scars or traumas left on the psyche which mark where the feelings have been wounded, hard scar tissue also protecting the sensitive spot. The event may be remembered, it may be repressed or 'forgotten' as being too painful to remember, or it may have occurred in the pre-memory stages of infancy whence it can be recovered only with the greatest difficulty.

The pre-memory period is the period before the brain has developed sufficiently for memories to be recalled. In fact it seems that even pre-birth events are recorded, and this accounts for the ability to recall the memory of these events with the aid of abreaction drugs, hypnosis and dreams.

The importance of traumas in the context of the inner work is that they compel us to feel, think or behave irrationally in respect of the particular areas of their effects. In this way they oppose our attempts to control the mind. But because their effects come from below the threshold of consciousness, people often need persuading that memories of a seemingly uneventful and fairly happy childhood are of no consequence when hunting down the causes of adult behaviour or tracing the roots of thoughts which disturb meditation. Behind happy memories may lie a mass of painful events which have been thrust away into forgetfulness; for the upbringing of a normal and happy child is necessarily associated with the rewards and punishments of hygiene training, with pleasures and pains, and with events like quarrelling parents. It is even possible for a person to say that he had a happy childhood only because he was unaware that life could be any better than the hell he was in. And in some cases there are those shocking events when a child discovers that it is adopted or that it was unwanted—events that may be repressed and whose memory may be recovered later in life through dream.

The following is an example of a dream that recovered an event in early infancy which, in later life, resulted in an irrational fear of leopards in a situation where leopards were common and, as dangerous animals, also justified a rational fear.

I dreamed I was very small and was lying on the floor behind the back of a sofa. My father's head appeared over the backrest and he snarled at me. My father had grey hair, brushed close to his head, a clipped grey moustache, and grey-blue eyes. He was an army officer, shell-shocked in World War I. In my childhood, if I disturbed him, he would snarl and roar at me, and he terrified me. As soon as I saw the similarity between his head and a leopard's, the irrational fear of leopards disappeared.

Painful traumas which are repressed attract much attention because their presence can be inferred from their effects, but the facts are difficult to recover. Indeed, the recovery of the facts may go a long way towards healing the trauma. When there seems no hope of recovering the memory, it is often possible to gain considerable mileage by assuming that an event of such and such a sort must have occurred which would account for these effects. However, one needs to be warned of the danger of inventing a trauma, such as being sexually abused by a parent, not because it really happened, but because one wanted it to happen. The trauma in such a case, as Freud discovered, is not so much the event, as it is the guilt at having desired it.

It also has to be noted that pleasant events, though easily remembered, are sometimes almost as traumatic as unpleasant ones in the way they distort later responses to life situations. An over-indulged child is as deeply traumatized as a deprived one. A particular holiday or birthday party may imprint an image of happiness on a child's mind such that, without being aware of it, the adult is constantly seeking to recapture that moment.

Why should painful events have such a devastating effect on individuals, and why more effect on some than on others? Some sort of answer may lie in one of those unexplainable facts of life which is so well documented that, as a fact, it has to be accepted.

This is the fact that a child coming to birth is extraordinarily sensitive to the manner of its reception—a sensitivity that may extend from the moment of birth to around age twelve. If it is received with welcoming care, gentleness and affection, it promptly begins to form a relationship with its mother or nurse, and it is this which lays the foundations of its later confidence in relating to people and to the external world in general. But if its first experience of life is of neglect, harsh treatment, discomfort and pain, it may interpret life as being so unpleasant that it rejects any form of relationship and retreats into an in-turned world of private fantasy. Typically, any attempt to disturb such fantasy life results in a tantrum of screaming violence. An extreme turning away from life into a private world can lead to autism.[1]

As with so many psychological patterns, the fortunately rare cases of extreme autism are like exaggerated caricatures of tendencies shared in some degree by millions. By seeing the caricatures, we become aware of those tendencies in ourselves.

What determines why one child goes autistic, while another child subjected to similar treatment develops normally is an unanswered question. One could speculate that a human soul coming to birth for the first time would be extremely sensitive to circumstances, while a soul with several lives behind it would know that 'life's like that' and so be able to ride any trouble that came its way. However, the point to be noted is the fragility of any child's capacity to adapt to the human condition.

When a child starts with the firm foundation of a good relationship with its mother, and its exposure to the harsh side of life comes in so balanced a way that it strengthens rather than weakens its confidence in itself, then it will probably develop a robust ego which will carry it through life's rough patches without damage. But any less confident child retains more of its initial fragility. Events like the illness or death of a parent, parental divorce, adoption, a violent attack on itself and witnessing violence on another can so damage the as yet delicate ego that the child reverts to infantilism. Even though the child will again grow up, some of the traumatic effects will remain.

---

[1] *The Empty Fortress*, Bruno Bettelheim; Free Press, 1967.

Those who have never suffered in this way find it difficult to understand and sympathize with the problems of their more sensitive fellows. Whether understood or not, the effects are uncomfortably real. We can see that the delicacy of the child's psyche, which makes it vulnerable to damage by bright lights and loud noises at the moment of birth, is the same phenomenon as the sensitivity of the adult who breaks down under the stress of explosions and violence in war. One of the most fertile areas of trauma is sex. But trauma is by no means limited to physical events. Fear, shame, guilt, failure and disappointment can be similarly damaging to a person's sense of identity and worth and the self-confidence which goes with them.

As an example one can quote the case of James, the eleven-year-old son of a London schoolmaster studying at a Catholic school. He came first in the eleven-plus exam, getting nearly a hundred per cent marks in most subjects. On the basis of this he was offered a full scholarship to a famous public school. The Catholic headmaster and James's father decided to refuse the scholarship because the other school was Protestant. Next term James fell to the bottom of the class and never shone at school again. This completely changed the life opportunities which were open to him. He lost confidence in his intellectual abilities and became somewhat uncertain at expressing himself both in speech and writing. Although he had a much more interesting and adventurous life than academic success might have given him, at one point becoming the founder-editor of a prestigious design magazine, it was not until he was over forty that a series of dreams suggested the connection between his lack of self-confidence and the devastating shock and disappointment deriving from his father's decision. Even then, he was reluctant to accept the fact because it would have meant seeing his father in a negative light.

Not every disappointment need take so long to resolve. Peter, an English boy of fifteen, had twice fallen ill on the last day of term at a public school, so that to his intense disappointment he had to spend the holidays in the isolation ward of a hospital. His headmaster then helped him to see that he was terrified of his father—something he had not known because it had seemed that that was what life was like. In fact, it was as if his psyche had said, 'You may feel disappointed, boy, but you will be happier this way,' while pushing him into hospital.

Unknown to Peter, the headmaster arranged with Peter's mother that he would be kept away from home during the holidays—glorious holidays that he spent with an aunt in Wales and grandparents in Scotland.

Over the next two years, his position in class rose from between seventeenth and twentieth in a class of twenty-three to around sixth, and he passed the Oxford and Cambridge Schools Certificate with six credits. So well was the secret of the arrangement kept that it was not until he was nearly forty that Peter learned what his headmaster had done for him.

In another case, Anita had reached the age when, as she well knew, she was to go to a boarding school. It so happened that her mother, who was divorced, remarried at just that time. The girl developed epilepsy. It seemed that the girl had unconsciously interpreted these circumstances to mean that she was being sent away because her mother no longer wanted her. The result was that the illness immediately brought her much attention from her frantic mother, which is the compensatory effect of many psychosomatic illnesses.

However, on the other side of the account, the drugs which controlled the epilepsy and made her 'feel like a cabbage' also seemed to hold up her development so that for several years she behaved more childishly than was normal for her age.

Another sort of trauma happened to John, a boy of twelve, who one day looked up his mother's skirts when she was bending over. A few days later, his mother suffered a miscarriage and was rushed off to hospital with a dangerous haemorrhage, while the children were sent to stay with an uncle.

Under such circumstances, a child's reactions can take a primitive form, as illustrated by the ravings of the Old Testament Prophets when Israel was attacked, and the explanation was given that Israel had sinned and Jehovah was angry. When something goes wrong, it is assumed that one is being punished for one's sins. Something *had* gone wrong; the mother's serious illness threatened the boy's basic security. The miscarriage connected in his mind with the guilt of having seen up his mother's skirts. Therefore he felt that in some inscrutable way he was responsible for the miscarriage. He reverted to an infantile need for the reassurance of cuddling; and the puberty which had begun normally at twelve was arrested until he was over seventeen.

Traumas of this sort, which have shaken the foundations of a growing child's self-confidence, may take a long time to erode even with patience and understanding.

By contrast, there is a class of traumas which may quickly submit to an understanding of the facts. Fear of the dark and of thieves often derives from the parental practice of stealing quietly into the bedroom of a sleeping child and gently slipping in a hand to see if the bed is wet. The child is often half aware of what is happening, but interprets it as the stealthy movement of a thief—particularly when the child is a boy and the fear of castration complicates the issue. Another occasion is when the visitor is Granny who has removed her dentures before retiring and looks like the archetypal witch of fairy stories with her chin meeting her nose. This simple perception can go a long way to remove night fears with their attendant nightmares.

Similarly, dreams of being chased or carried off by giants derive from the child's perception of its parents as huge and powerful. The image may then be aroused by any situation in which the person feels he is powerless, but the fear belongs to the child. Nightmares of this sort can often be dealt with by seeing that what was a rational fear for the infant is irrational and unnecessary for the adult. Indeed, this formula has many applications in later life, as when one can look back on a shameful episode and say, 'I am no longer that silly young fool.' One breaks the identification and can stop cringing with shame.

As we have seen, children kept unaware of adult sexuality tend to assume, by a sort of irrational logic, that adults are not interested in the areas of erotic interest which they forbid to children. In such a setting, a child who inadvertently walks in on parents performing the sexual act may suffer a severe shock because it cannot relate what its parents are doing to its view of its parents. Depending on the child's age, the parents may be thought to be fighting—a frightening event for most children—or to be doing something utterly disgusting. Even the atmosphere of highly aroused desire can be disturbing to a child. Such events can give rise to a degree of neurotic conflict because the child is presented with mutually contradictory stimuli: the parental command, 'Thou shalt not be interested', and the instinctive prompting which says 'Look'. Its interpretation of the sexual act as fighting may therefore be more than just a misunderstanding; it can also reflect its own conflict. Dreams of fighting, besides representing any state of conflict, can also refer both to this fairly common trauma and to its effects as representing the conflict between imposed standards and natural instincts.

Another common trauma occurs in societies where male genitals are customarily concealed, even from other men. Under such circumstances, a boy's chance view of adult male genitals, especially if erect, gives him a standard of size against which he measures his own and which he may never have the opportunity to revise. Even though he grows normally at puberty, the relative measurements remain fixed in his mind— a phenomenon which is common in regard to many comparisons of scale between childhood's memories of objects and their appearance to the same person as an adult. Though this may seem ridiculous to men habituated to male nudity in changing rooms and army camps, it is in fact a common trauma amongst those who are not. The corresponding effect of a view of male genitals on small girls normally lasts only till their first sexual experience but it can extend into an irrational desire for sex with a man with a proportionately huge organ. In men, however, the early demonstration of their own smallness leaves them with a lasting sense of organ inadequacy which gets perpetuated by being linked to the common anxieties that afflict males in regard to their virility, acceptability and capacity to satisfy a woman—anxieties that are not always removed by sexual experience.

Dreams relating to this sort of subject can have a significance deeper than just reassuring a man as to the size of his genitals. Often, a man's general sense of inadequacy has got projected or hooked on to his genitals, so that any current stimulus to his anxiety may get transferred to his sense of physical inadequacy. Indeed, our purpose is not to reassure such a man about his genital adequacy, but to break his self-identification with mere physical characteristics, and to persuade him to find his identity in the Self.

This is another area where the importance of flexibility has to be emphasized. We cannot lay down the law and say that all problems can be solved inwardly by understanding, so that acting them out is a second-rate method. Nor can we say that freedom from traumas and inhibitions can be attained only by acting out one's freedom. The world population is at all stages of human development in all parts of the world, so that some people arrive at understanding and maturity only through action and some by direct perception. Even in one individual, there are areas that can be cleared by perception and areas where things have to be worked out in practice. However, one has to be careful not to allow the common fear of getting one's hands dirty to stop one from action where perception is not enough.

These are examples of events associated with childhood which affect an adult's view of one of the most important areas of his or her life: sex. Despite world society's move towards greater sexual freedom, repressions, inhibitions and traumas are still very much with us. People still go through their lives believing themselves 'abnormal' because their thoughts do not conform to what they have been taught to believe are everyone's 'normal' thoughts, and they still condemn others as mad or perverted because they have dared to express ideas that are not respectable by current standards.

What has happened in society seems to be less of a liberation from the old sexual standards than a reaction against them. The development of contraceptive technology permitted the enjoyment of sex without fear of conception. Few people would listen to the voices which said that sex was not merely a pleasurable act to be indulged freely when the social consequences were removed. Promiscuity, therefore, went rampant in established society. Large numbers of the young opted out on sex and drugs, demonstrating by their undirected drifting, slovenly ways and low level of mentation—their avowed aim of spiritual liberation notwithstanding—that unrestricted sexual indulgence drains the psyche of the energy which has raised human intelligence above that of the animals and must be further harnessed if mankind is to rise further into full humanity.

Certainly, this new generation does not blush when speaking of sex, nor are they consumed with the repressed curiosity that seemed to have befuddled many in the Victorian era. They have experimented with all the 'perversions', they can do anything sexual. But, in doing it, they have missed the point. They have not done it to free their intelligence for greater understanding of their human state. They have done it in revolt against (admittedly inadequate) social norms. The result is that they have deprived themselves of the psychic benefits brought about by the imposition of those norms, namely, the heightening of intelligence and the enhancement of self-awareness. We need better norms, better understanding of what social conditioning is aimed at, and better methods of training our infants and educating our children. But until these better methods are evolved, we achieve nothing by throwing the old ones away. We merely revert to animality.

However, even though many people found the phenomenon offensive, it is a fact that this phase of sexual freedom has cleaned much of the dirt out of social attitudes towards sex. In the context of personal attitudes in the inner work, such cleaning is the foundation upon which the success of meditative work will depend, for one cannot build on land from which jungle growth has not been cleared.

Few people will have difficulty in recognizing the state of mind of the twelve-year-old boy who, wishing to instruct a friend in the mystery of the sex act, said, 'Think of the dirtiest thing you could do.' Even though later experience may clear away much of that conditioned sense of dirt, it will not eradicate the patterns imposed on the subconscious mind. No matter what freedom a man may allow himself under the stimulus of Eros, invariably distinctions are drawn between what we may do and how much under what circumstances, what we may say privately and what in open society, what is suited to monosexual society and what to mixed society. There is the dirty joke voice, the flat clinical voice, the daring voice, the 'let's be frank' voice, the polite society voice, the embarrassed mumble, and the firm 'let's change the subject'. Then there is the man who likes to shock, and the man who insists on telling everyone about his piles. Not one of them is natural. Each tells us that sex and its associated organs belong to a special subject. And so they do; but not for the reason that they are dirty or sinful.

Our attitude towards sex is, therefore, one of the most important and frequent subjects to appear in dream. These attitudes are not formed only on what everyone recognizes as directly genital experience. The parental attitude towards the anal and genital zones—anything below the navel— towards lavatories, bathrooms and underwear, all go towards forming our attitudes towards sex, sexual organs, and the substitute symbols of sex.

Freud's contributions in this field are of great importance.

Perhaps the most important lesson to be learned from him is the need to let the mind associate freely in the region of sexual symbolism. On the other hand, the most important caution to be given is not to follow Freud in his mistaken treatment of parallels as equations. Sitting in meditation need not be 'brooding at stool', nor need it be an attempt to get back into the mother's womb. Dreams of defecation need not refer to anal eroticism, but to voiding psychic material considered as inner dirt, and so bringing it out into consciousness where it can be dealt with and eventually washed away. A dream of sex with the mother need not refer to the Oedipus complex or to incestuous guilt, but can represent recognition that the mother is also a woman with whom sexual relations are possible, even though socially inappropriate, and that a man who has matured to the point where he is truly free from his mother can see her as just another woman whom he may or may not like.

It is, therefore, always advisable to start interpretation by trying out the keys of sexual symbolism. Since there is scarcely anything which cannot be given a sexual slant, there is scarcely a dream that cannot yield a sexual interpretation. One can remain content with such an interpretation only if it seems to provide a previously unknown insight into the dreamer's nature, and which the dreamer himself accepts as being meaningful to him. If this is not the case, then other keys can be tried until the conditions of a successful interpretation are satisfied. Constant practice of this 'descent' into areas customarily excluded from spiritual contemplation has the effect of eroding the fears and disgusts which normally inhibit the mind. Freedom to move between the depths and heights of the psyche is essential to the integration of man's many parts into a whole that reflects the wholeness of being.

Anxiety Dreams

Most people are familiar with dreams which reflect a state of anxiety. The dreamer finds himself late for an appointment, missing trains and buses, unprepared for examinations, not fully dressed when guests arrive, losing his way, etc. In many cases, such a theme is recurrent, which usually means, with reference to the dreamer's personal dream idiom, that any current anxiety situation gets expressed in standard terms which spell anxiety; but there may be no connection between the situation which provoked the anxiety and the dream images which spell anxiety. Interpretation is, therefore, more concerned with identifying the waking situation which has triggered the anxiety dream than with analysis of the dream details.

However, when a series of such dreams is remembered, further inquiry should be made in the attempt to identify the early life period when this anxiety pattern was established, and to encourage the dreamer to discover what the basic anxiety is. For instance, it is very common for young people to feel themselves unprepared for the challenges of adult life. They wonder whether they will be adequate to the situations into which they will be thrown. The youngster who eagerly states that he is just longing to get into life and take responsibility is often repressing his anxieties and his sense of inadequacy, and will be a candidate for just this type of recurrent anxiety dream. Since school examinations or catching the school bus represent preparation for adult life, to be unprepared for examinations or to miss the bus, easily comes to represent doubt as to one's adequacy in meeting new situations, both in youth and in later life.

The cure for this sort of anxiety does not lie in forcing oneself to work harder so as to be better prepared for the particular event. To do this would be to fall victim to the current glorification of competitiveness and success, which leads only to a self-confidence based on the unstable ground of personal achievement. On such ground, anxiety is perpetuated, for in a competitive world there is no assurance that a successful man will not suffer failure at the instance of a more successful man.

Self-confidence must be built on the unshakeable certainty of the Self, not on fragile ego-achievements. This does not deny the practical need of young people to build a measure of personality with which they achieve a working relationship with life situations. They need to prove themselves; and anxiety can be the spur that drives them to achievement. The 'young soul' needs encouragement to conquer its anxieties on their own level, in the same way that the new-born infant needs to be reassured that it is welcomed and loved before it dare venture into a positive relationship with its guardians. But when adults continue to pursue the same aims of adaptation as are suited to the growth of adolescents, they tend to remain adolescent in outlook.

The aim of the adult should be akin to that of the samurai swordsman who, realizing that sooner or later he would meet his equal in swordsmanship, set about to conquer his fear of death. An adult should be able to rest in the calm certainty of his human essence, neither thinking himself the greater on account of his knowledge, achievements or abilities, nor thinking himself the less on account of his ignorance or failures. This is not a withdrawal into moronic apathy. A man who is essentially sure of himself is, in fact, better adapted to life than a man who supports himself on qualities of personality alone. He admits his limitations because he feels himself no less a man on their account and, because he can admit his ignorance, he is free to seek the knowledge he needs without embarrassment. He also develops in human relationships because he neither needs to shield himself nor seeks support and reassurance.

A man who seeks such certainty treats anxieties as indicators to components of his being which require his attention. They can be regarded as conditioned responses, which were both natural and necessary to him in childhood and adolescence, but which become unnecessary to a man whose certainty is rooted in what stands beyond success and failure, beyond praise and blame. In order to combat such conditioning, however, he will need to challenge the assumptions or premises which provided the rationale for its imposition.

Many of these premises derive from instinctual behaviour patterns common to most animals, behaviour which is related to the evolutionary doctrine of survival of the fittest. Among animals, the strongest and most aggressive tend to claim the best food, to win the fairest mates, to rule the largest territory, to perpetuate their kind, and to survive the longest. Mankind overcame the brute strength of animals with intelligence and skill, but remained essentially brutish. The same instinctual principles that rule animals now rule the world of monetary economics. Most economically powerful and aggressive people lay claim to all the greatly valued things of the world, and world society continues to accept the value system which puts the possessors of these things at the top of the heap. This forms the success image, the competitiveness, the 'doing well' with which our youths are indoctrinated. The fear that they may not be equal to a competitive world produces their anxiety, and the continued acceptance of those standards into adult life perpetuates their vulnerability to anxiety aroused by derivative situations.

Anxiety can sometimes drive one into unwise actions. As an example, one can quote the case of Ananda who was in charge of an ashram in a remote hill area. He was thrown into a state of acute anxiety by the threat of governmental interference in the running of the ashram, which he feared would destroy what it stood for. As a result, he planned to send letters appealing for help to all the influential people he knew and were in a position to intervene. Before he actually wrote any letters, he had the following dream.

He found himself in the local post office, dispatching registered letters. On leaving the post office, he was amazed to see a caravan of Bactrian camels sweeping down the hill road, as if coming from an earlier age, when such camels might have come from China, across Tibet and down the old pilgrim route which ran past his village. Then he saw a nomad's tent pitched on the other side of the road. He crossed the road and entered the tent. Inside was an elderly man, very erect and stern, wearing homespun woollen clothes, dyed a soft red and blue. He was evidently the leader of the caravan. Looking straight at Ananda, the man said: 'Don't do these things. You will make for yourself inner enemies.'

Shamed to the core by the impact of these words from

such an impressive figure, Ananda left the tent and turned back to the road. The caravan had passed, but proudly standing in the middle of the road was a beautiful Bactrian camel, large, woolly and black. From his head, two new white cotton ropes trailed back behind him, one on each side. Ananda stepped between the ropes and took them up, one in each hand. Promptly, the camel soared into the air, taking Ananda with him.

On waking, the immediate association to this remarkable camel was a favourite rendering of a verse from the Sufi poet and mystic, Ibn Arabi: 'Love is the guide and love is the goal / where'er love's camels turn, the one true way is there.'

Thus, in one 'big dream' Ananda was both scolded for letting his anxiety run away with him, and then shown that he should follow the transcendental path of love.

In the event, the threat of government interference came to nothing.

The 'inner enemies' refer to the strengthening of the sense of dependence on friends and relations for one's security, instead of cultivating the sense of total dependence on the Spirit. If turning to people in the world for help becomes a habit, that habit is an 'inner enemy'.

8

Out-of-the-body Dreams

There is an occult belief that the 'subtle body' invariably separates from the physical during sleep. I am not convinced that it is invariably the case. The sleeping awareness is certainly in a state of dissociation from the body, but this is not quite the same thing as being spatially separate. However, even if it were to be so, it would be unimportant in respect of the majority of dreams in which there is neither awareness of exteriorization nor any dream content which, under analysis, discloses evidence of exteriorization.

The value to the beginner of an experience of being out of the body is that it gives him a personally convincing demonstration of the falsity of the materialist thesis that the entire universe is nothing but its material components. It demonstrates to him that he can exist and retain his awareness of existing apart from the body, and that this, without further evidence, provides him with rational and experiential grounds for reassessing whatever views he holds as to the significance of this world and the significance of the mystical philosophies. For some people it sets the seal on a previously held belief.

It needs emphasizing, however, that an experience of exteriorization is convincing only to the person concerned. It is not evidential to anyone else, except perhaps to a person with developed psychic vision who, in any case, needs no convincing. Current medical and psychological science treats out-of-the-body experiences as hallucination, and a large part of the world population finds it convenient to agree because they feel threatened by anything which shakes their habitually timid outlook. However, in the modern world there is much talk of 'Lucid Dreaming', which appears to be the same thing by another name.

To be convincing, such a demonstration requires that the person be awake either throughout the exteriorization or at some point in it. However, even when he feels himself to be fully awake, as often as not it happens that some of the things he looks at appear different from what they would be when seen in physical waking. Obviously, he can recognize such differences only when he finds himself in familiar surroundings. In strange surroundings, or in surroundings familiar only to the exteriorized state, he cannot know whether they are purely visionary or whether they have material counterparts and, if so, how much of what he sees is objectively stable and how much changes.

In any of these cases, the degree of objective agreement between what is seen in the embodied waking state and what is seen in the disembodied waking state seems to turn largely on the degree of 'awakeness' when exteriorized. A lesser degree of awakeness leads to a greater degree of dream content intruding into the vision of the observer. As awakeness decreases, so dream content increases, until the dream images cease to have any recognizable connection with the material surroundings.

Between the extremes of fully waking and fully dreaming exteriorization there is, therefore, an area of mixed waking and dreaming where the dream content tends to get projected onto the 'screen' of objective reality. At the waking end of the scale perhaps only one or two objects may be seen as changed. At the dreaming end, the entire surroundings may be changed. For instance, in the former case, everything in a familiar room may appear normal, except that the wooden floor has been changed to one of patterned stone. In the latter case, the fireplace appears as an altar, an existing wardrobe appears as a door, the glass window panes have been replaced by carved panels, and a flowering tree has replaced a lamp stand, while other features of the room are vague. So strange is the setting, that it is only on reflection that the dreamer can recognize that the dream scene had been imposed on waking reality.

Anyone learning to operate in the subtle worlds is more concerned to prevent the intrusion of dream content than to remember it and then analyse it. He has to learn to assert the power of his waking awareness over the projected psychic content of the dreaming awareness and so to force the apparently changed objects to go back to their normal form. However, I am not concerned here with the techniques and disciplines for conscious operation in the exteriorized state. I am concerned with inquiry into the significance of dream content, whether seen as superimposed on objective reality or without reference to an objective screen, and whether the observer welcomes its appearance or attempts to repress it.

In the long run, intelligent inquiry into the significance of dream content is more consonant with the aims of the inner path than is the deliberate effort to see the undistorted objectivity of the subtle worlds. Seeing in the subtle worlds is not so very different from seeing in the physical world. Our concern is less with the seen than with the Seer. 'When the mind is at rest, the Seer stands in his own nature.'[1] The problem is to set the mind at rest. If the mind is full of repressed psychic content, it will not come to rest of its own accord. As soon as the waking focus relaxes, the repressed content leaps out and projects itself to appear as if objective. This is why people who plunge into intense meditation without preparation are liable to experience 'horrible' visions. They are horrible only to someone who is horrified by the baseness of his own subconscious mind when its content is projected in vision, in the same way that we have bad dreams or nightmares.

This work on dreams aids us both in bringing the mind to rest and in gaining a view of life which is undistorted by the value systems imposed on us by our upbringing. If the operator in the subtle worlds ignores the confusion that reigns in the unconscious levels of his psyche, he will remain the same confused man in the inner worlds as he is in the outer. Nor will he be able to progress further in spiritual insight than the equivalent stage which his psychological confusion would permit him to reach when leaving the physical body at death. It is true that one can gain the detached freedom from good and bad by other means, but those means tend to be associated with paths which stress transcendence at the expense of compassion.

As with meditation, it often happens that the process of exteriorization is accompanied by dreams or half-waking experiences which frighten the dreamer, particularly when it is happening for the first time and he does not know what to expect. If his breathing appears to have stopped, he thinks he is dying, and if he cannot move his body, he thinks he has

---

[1] The *Yoga Sutras* of Patanjali.

had a paralytic stroke. Few people can contemplate such unexpected symptoms with equanimity. Many people, therefore, panic and, awakening to find themselves as normal as before, describe what has happened as a frightening dream.

In normal sleep, in states of deep meditation, and sometimes during exercises in physical relaxation, the body goes into various degrees of catalepsy in which a conscious effort is required to move a limb. In sleep and in deep meditation, breathing is also affected. For a precise description one would have to go to a neurologist, but for present purposes the following description of what happens to breathing should suffice. In the waking state, breathing is partly volitional and partly under the control of the autonomic nervous system. The volitional part of it is what allows us to control our breath so that we can talk in long sentences, rather than in gasps, and allows us to hold our breath under water. But when we fall asleep, the control of breathing is taken over by the autonomic nervous system entirely, so that breathing continues without interruption. In passing into sleep, the transition of control from one part of the brain to the other is usually smooth. In passing from a meditative state of the waking mind into deep meditation, a similar transition occurs: volitional breathing is handed over to the sympathetic system, centred in the medulla oblongata. In both sleep and meditation, this change is associated with a dissociation of mind from body which is not necessarily spatial. But whereas in sleep the awareness of the person passes into relative unconsciousness, in meditation the waking awareness of the mind remains while the body falls asleep. In this case, the transitional stage is often marked by a momentary blurring of the focus of awareness. The transition may not be smooth, especially when the observer is not accustomed to it. A pause is apt to occur in which breathing is controlled neither by one part of the brain nor by the other, so that it appears to stop. If the person panics at this unusual phenomenon, he wakes immediately and breathes as before. But if he remains calm, the autonomic system takes over, as in sleep, while his awareness 'stands in its own nature'. The physiological condition of the body may not be precisely the same as in sleep, but is very close to it.

The transition can be witnessed without specific reference to meditation if the intention to stay awake is strongly held while the body is allowed to relax, as if for sleep. It similarly occurs during exteriorization when, for practical purposes, the body remains asleep and cataleptic. Sometimes, however, there is a transitional stoppage of breath during exteriorization which gives rise to the frightening dreams mentioned earlier.

The difference in rhythm between the breathing of the normal waking state, even in repose, and that of sleep is known to everyone, and many people know that sleep can be induced by synchronizing one's breath with that of a person sleeping close by. Yogis maintain that every one of the inner states of consciousness has its characteristic breathing rhythm, and it seems that some of the many breathing exercises prescribed by the Yoga system may originally have been patterned on the observed breath rhythms of people in deep meditation and samadhi. On the same imitative principle by which sleep may be induced, it seems that yogis hope to induce samadhi by controlling their own breath rhythm on the pattern of one in samadhi. The practice is not recommended without the guidance of a teacher.

9

Reincarnation

A review of the public claims in support of reincarnation is a necessary introduction to a discussion of past life references, which often come into the dreams of people working on the spiritual path. Serious Seekers are concerned to keep their vision as free as possible from the distortions caused by fear, desire, superstition, literalistic interpretations of traditional teachings, and the fantasies that arise out of all these. They will certainly try to distinguish between what they believe to be a factual past life reference and a therapeutic fantasy.

A significant difference between the therapeutic fantasy and the authentic dream is that dream images arise from or are thrust up by the levels of the psyche of which we are normally unconscious. Those levels are, by definition, free from the corrupting influences of the ego which rules the conscious mind. We can, therefore, place greater trust in dreams when they indicate a previous life as the source of a trauma, than we can in the vision of a psychic or the guided imagery of a psychologist.

Western attitudes towards the doctrine of reincarnation have remained dismissive, in spite of (even because of) the current vogue for having unconfirmable visions of past lives under some sort of psychological guidance, known as past life therapy. It is also thought of as an exotic, Oriental doctrine, which is suspect for that very reason.

In fact, reincarnation was probably as common a belief among the pre-Christian tribal communities of Europe as it is amongst tribals anywhere, because, often on account of dreams, such people frequently identify new-born children with deceased relatives.

Indeed, the pre-existence of the soul and, by extension, reincarnation, was forbidden to be taught by the early Christian church subsequent only to the promulgation of the anathemas against Origen in AD 553. Even now, the Catholic church does not condemn belief in reincarnation, and there appear to be doubts whether the anathemas against Origen should be accepted, for the Pope of the time opposed them. Many of the early Church Fathers accepted the doctrine.[1]

For me personally, reincarnation is a simple fact of existence which explains the cumulative effect of life experiences, and so the differences in character between individuals coming to birth, differences which are not explainable by the common division into the effects of nature and nurture—genetics and environment.

The process by which the soul or human monad takes birth in a series of bodies permits an accumulation of the experience of many lives, such that a monad that begins with an unrealized potentiality for self-awareness can become the central essence of a completely evolved human being.

The ordinary ego-centred individual may find it difficult to grasp the significance of a harvest of experience which is

---

[1] *Reincarnation: An East West Anthology*, Head and Cranston; Theosophical Publishing House, 1961.

neither the events nor the memories of events, but is the sum of all the effects of the events on the witness. This difficulty is related to another one, that of understanding how a life of which one has no memory and which seems to have been lived by someone else can in any sense be 'mine'. Still less is the doctrine found acceptable that there is a causal connection between events in that other person's life and my suffering in this life.

It is in this connection that the psychological discovery that the forgotten events of childhood continue to affect adult behaviour is of great importance, for it provides an example of how the forgotten events of past lives may continue to affect us in this life.

Here it needs to be mentioned that it is no more necessary to believe in reincarnation in order to follow the spiritual path, than it is necessary to know about the circulation of blood (a late discovery) in order to live. However, both happen to be facts, and reincarnation is a fact that explains much about the evolution of the individual and so throws light on the meaning of life.

This issue is again confused by what is taken to be another fact: the self-aware human monad is not an indestructible, permanent identity, any more than the temporary identity of the person in this life. Although (in Buddhist terms) it can be represented as the thread on which one Self's separate lives are strung, and although it is capable of looking back upon the series, as did the Buddha at his attainment, yet it is in itself but a spark of the parent flame of universal awareness. Like a spark, it is temporarily separate from its source, and is capable of falling back into it with total annihilation of its separate existence.

It is for this reason that people who are attempting the

discovery of this transcendental aspect of the human identity may, like some Buddhists, deny the whole doctrine of reincarnation. For while it is true that in the same state they are now in, they were previously identified with other incarnations, just as they are factually identified with the present one, by their denial they wish to make it true that their ultimate identity is with that universal source which was never born and which never dies. Properly handled, this is not self-deception, but a valid method for breaking down a false identity in order to find the true one.

It must be emphasized that this last, transcendental identity which is found is not simply the last person in the series of lives, nor is it the evolved monad which has reaped the harvest of those lives. The series of lives has provided the means by which the potentialities of the experiencing monad have been realized to the point where it becomes capable of transcending itself.

The parallel drawn between the forgetting of childhood's traumas and the forgetting of past lives—a very approximate parallel—can be treated as a pragmatic truth only if we have examples of the recovery of the memory of past lives in the same way that we have of the recovery of traumatic events.

There are well researched and documented accounts of people, particularly children, who have detailed memories of a previous life and have been able to identify the places they lived in and the people who were previously their family relations and associates.[2] The 'official' view is that these phenomena, if they are to be taken seriously at all, prove only that the memories of a dead person can become available to a presently living one. They do not prove an identity

---

[2] *Twenty Cases of Suggestive Reincarnation*, Ian Stevenson; University Press of Virginia, 1980.

between the two persons. Obviously, if the person is defined by the body, then the dead body of a thirty-year-old man and the live body of a child of six cannot be the same person. We get a different reading when the person is identified as the Self, Soul, or self-conscious entity residing in the body during life and leaving it at death. It then becomes a straightforward matter to accept the fact of such memories as evidence for reincarnation.

Previous lives in this category are seldom very remarkable. There may be a strong emotional aura about the death at the end of the previous life—by accident, murder or suicide—which suggests a reason for the memory being intense enough to be carried over. They also tend to be quick rebirths, such that even previous parents may still be alive. The subtle world phenomena associated with rebirth make it more likely that memories will be carried over with a quick rebirth than with the more normal pattern of a delayed one. It is rare for this sort of memory, which is recalled by the waking mind, to go beyond the one previous life.

As Freud discovered, all sense experience appears to be recorded in memory below the threshold of waking consciousness. Only a relatively small part of it is normally available for recall in the waking state, but the record itself seems to be indestructible. Experience with dream recall and with drug-induced and hypnotic regression shows that the memory of previous lives is also stored in the unconscious mind. However, it should hardly need stating that the main value of these directly remembered and confirmed previous life experiences lies in the fact of their being confirmed, for the lives themselves seldom seem to have any world-shaking significance, as mentioned earlier. The other modes in which it is claimed to recall the memories of previous lives for the most part yield results which, at the best, give only personal conviction. However, some of them deserve comment, if only because they have been popularized.

The first of these methods is typified by the American psychic and healer Edgar Cayce who is reported to have diagnosed diseases in clients and to have prescribed medicines while in trance. Occasionally he would give 'life readings' for a client in which he would describe traumatic events in the client's previous lives which, he suggested, were responsible for the physical and psychic maladies the client was suffering from. This information was reported to have given considerable relief to the clients.

Criticisms were made that there was a common pattern in many, if not all of these reported lives. It was alleged that in nearly all cases the first of the reported lives was supposed to have been during the American Civil War, the second in the War of American Independence, in the third the client had been a member of the French court of Louis XIV at Versailles, there was then a big jump to a life in 'ancient Egypt', and finally one in Persia. In defence, it was said that Cayce was reporting only important lives, but that there were many less important ones in the gaps. However, even allowing that the mass psychosis of war and revolution provides a fertile soil for traumatic events, it would be a rash claim that events of great personal significance are restricted to such times.

It may also be remembered that Versailles and ancient Egypt were highly popular amongst post-Blavatsky theosophists as the scenes for the previous lives about which there was much fantasizing.

None of this can be accepted as convincing evidence of objective reporting on previous lives. Diseases whose causation may lie in the traumatic events of previous lives qualify as psychosomatic diseases. But the nature of psychosomatic disease is such that even a cure brought about through the disclosure of the traumatic event from which it started does not validate the historical nature of the reported event. What matters here is not the literal truth of the statement but what may be called its psychological truth, namely, the description of an event which so adequately symbolizes the psychological causation that it is effective as a cure. Here it is relevant to note that while a girl's fantasy of an incestuous affair with her father can cause as much of a guilt neurosis as if it had been physical, as Freud discovered, there are grounds for supposing that another sort of fantasy could cure a neurosis. In this case, the story of its being an event in a previous life makes it a personal myth—an account of something so deeply buried in the unconscious that it can be symbolized as a past life. The person feels that it corresponds to something very deep within himself. One should also remember that a dream of the fourteenth century is less likely to refer to a life at that time, than it does to events at age fourteen.

In fact, we can neither confirm nor deny the claims put forward on behalf of Cayce and others of the same sort regarding reincarnation. What we can say is that the chance of so many cases all occurring during those specific periods is so improbable that the claim detracts from the credibility of the stories' historical nature. But this in no way detracts from the claim for the therapeutic effectiveness of the total treatment.

When we turn to the reincarnation therapy presently in vogue, the case is no better. In place of one medium going into trance and speaking for all his clients, now we have the clients themselves being helped into a light trance or a state of mild dissociation in which visions are seen of events supposed to be in past lives, because the dress, architecture, etc., is identified with a particular historical period.

The same principle applies: the personal conviction of the client and the therapeutic effectiveness of the visions are in no way evidential of objectively historical events. All the reported visions could be produced by the psyche, the same dream artist who so brilliantly produces the images of our dreams out of the records with which our memory banks are stocked, records which, if we are to believe Jung, go far beyond the boundaries of our personal unconscious and into the collective memories of the race.

Anyone could retort that those banks also contain the records of all our previous lives. And so they do. But it takes more than a mild dose of hypnotic suggestion to push our capacity of dream vision over the threshold of this life's integration and to make the memories of those earlier lives available.

It is useful to contrast the differences between the way of looking at previous life experience, from the total identification with persons and events seen in the semi-hypnotic type of therapy currently in use, to the amazingly objective account of the death experience by Jung[3] in which, had he not been recalled, he would have met within the rock-cut temple the animated images of his previous lives, seen as distinct personalities with whom he was strangely familiar, a 'group soul' united in the search for the meaning of life. Together they would have decided to send down another representative to earth to continue the search. Yet another persona was to be added to the group's collection. Another house was to be built.

---

[3] *Memories, Dreams, Reflections*, C.G. Jung; Vintage, 1989.

Consider again the account of the Buddha's attainment, when he turned his mind to previous lives and, as a traveller who has climbed a high hill looks back upon the road he has travelled and sees, 'there I travelled, there I rested', so he looked back and saw the series of lives he had lived, now as a man of a particular caste and occupation, now as another. Yet he was above and beyond them, not one of them, not even the most recent one to which he would return. 'Broken the rafters. Sundered the ridge pole. No more shalt thou build house for me again.'

Even if the dreamer could be sure that such past life references were factual, the question would remain of what is to be gained from the knowledge of past lives in the context of the spiritual search.

We have already touched on one aspect of the question. People who are attempting to discover their true identity must simultaneously examine their self-identification with the racial, social and cultural characteristics of their present birth. Some of these characteristics are so deeply ingrained, in the form of attitudes, values and assumptions, that they are as hard to see as is water to the fish. It is, therefore, helpful to be jolted by a dream into the perception that many of one's unquestioned assumptions that seem so naturally true in the present cultural setting were certainly not true in a previous life when one belonged to a different and perhaps antagonistic race.

It might be supposed that this perception of the relativity of cultural norms might be arrived at by any ordinarily intelligent person by a mixture of thought and imagination; but that would lack the emotional impact which is what makes one begin to feel a stranger in both the present and previous cultural settings, and so become free to feel identified with one's truly human and spiritual roots.

Another gain lies in the sense of a meaningful continuity in life. One is not, as Jung felt himself to be, 'an historical fragment, an excerpt from which the preceding and succeeding text was missing'.[4] The urgency inherent in a single life effort may be reduced, but so is the numbing sense that a failure in this life is a failure forever. If one feels unready to aspire for the final goal, one can at least perform this life's tasks with the assurance that no effort is wasted. But anyone who looks on future lives as an opportunity for more fun and games is taking the sword by the blade and is likely to get hurt.

Dreams are not the only indicators of previous lives. There is the well-known phenomenon of déjà vu—the feeling 'I have been here before' and 'This has happened before'—which sometimes derives from previous life experience, as does an unexpected sense of affinity at first meeting with a stranger, but these and many others like them are fragile indications which will not carry much weight. One notes them and adds them to the sum of odd facts which taken by themselves are too small to be significant, yet when added together may amount to a formidable body of data that demands explanation.

For the person who has the courage and conviction to go his own way, these many modes in which subtle states of being impinge on us and enter our waking minds need no 'proof' of the material sort. The world is a richer place for their presence and, if one acts always in consonance with what one believes to be highest in oneself and one appreciates that nothing is to be regarded as a mistake if one has learned from it, then one can see that even a mistaken belief will

---

[4] Ibid.

support one for as long as it takes one to move on, when its collapse behind one will be of no importance.

When one is born into a family, a number of factors are unavoidably inherited. Firstly, there is the genetic inheritance from both parents; although there is room for considerable variation, the choice is limited. Then one is born into an ethnic and cultural environment which will impose values, standards, behavioural norms, and attitudes in general. There will be a mixture of the cultural norms of the race, as modified by social groups within the race. This cultural inheritance will be liable to include the friend/enemy convictions of the group towards neighbouring groups, and even the conditioned feeling of involvement in family feuds.

These various cultural identifications will be reinforced by the individual's psychological or instinctual need for the feeling of belonging and the support of group solidarity.

Finally, one comes to the characteristics of the person taking birth within the physical-cum-cultural framework, characteristics which must in some degree match the range of possibilities given by the framework. It is only in this last factor that one can find the roots of those strange feelings of affinity with particular people and places which suggest previous life connections.

In this context, I have a curious story to tell. Based on both personal and cultural affinities which began to surface even before I came to India, and backed by later dream evidence, I have reason to believe that for many lives I have been born in India, of which at least three were spent as a sadhu, the wandering mendicant monk. There was also the strange experience of finding my attention forcibly drawn to a particular place in a remote Christian cemetery where an English child had been buried before my birth in this body.

The attraction of my attention to the place in the cemetery preceded by a few months my meeting with an Englishman who was visiting his birthplace in India, and with whom I felt a strong though not very pleasant affinity. It was he who told me that his elder brother as a child had been buried in that spot. It was a reasonable assumption that I had attempted to obtain entry to an English birth in India, but the attempt failed with the death of the child. However, even the failure may have made it easier to obtain birth in Britain.

I was born in Edinburgh of a Scottish mother as the youngest of three children. One of my mother's stories which thrilled us children was the fairly well-known ghost story of Ticonderoga, which belongs to the 1750s. The chief character was one of her many Scottish ancestors. The story, as I remember her telling it, was that a fugitive came to the house of one of her ancestors in the West Highlands claiming sanctuary. If I ever knew it, I do not remember by what right he was able to claim protection by that ancient sacred custom, but the ancestor hid him in a cave on the hillside.

Then the pursuers arrived with the demand that the ancestor join them in the pursuit because the fugitive had killed one of his close relations, so it was now his duty to hunt him down and kill him. He joined them in the hopeless chase for the man he had himself hidden.

On his return, however, torn by conflicting loyalties and finding the man still there, he killed him. The story goes that for the next three nights the ghost appeared and solemnly announced, 'Remember me at Ticonderoga.' The name meant nothing to the ancestor.

Later, as so many penniless Scottish lairds did, he took up arms for the king and went to America with his sons. On the eve of battle (possibly the battle of 1758) he learned the name of the place: Ticonderoga, a French fort on the Canadian border. He called his sons and told them he would not survive the battle. He died the next day.

One might think that that would be the end of the story, but there is a sequel, which is my reason for telling the first part.

A few years ago, I heard from a relation in England that the man who was now feel titular chief of the clan was in trouble with the authorities over some tax affair, and could not shake off a cloud of depression that was shadowing him; and that my aged mother in one of her psychic moods had suspected that he was being 'got at' from the inner worlds on account of this same old tale of vengeance. It was a bit of family gossip in which I was not involved.

However, shortly afterwards I had the following dream experience. I was in the rather murky environment I have learned to associate with the lower levels of the world of the dead, and was confronting the vague and rather unpleasant presence of the person who was still planning his vengeance. With great clarity I said, 'You have no right to do this. The man was in an impossible position. Whatever he did would have been wrong.' Never have I felt so strongly the power of the spoken word.

I do not know the man for whom I spoke, nor do I have any sense of belonging to his clan. But I was struck by the nastiness and injustice of a vengeance that could be continued for so many generations. Yet at no point did I feel that I was acting on my own volition. I felt that I was being used by a greater power to stop this unjustified malice. And I could be used because of my connection by birth with that family, while I had no historical involvement with the feud.

It, therefore, appears that in taking a British birth and so getting the advantages of (at that time) a British upbringing, I became identified with the family history and its emotional content. Fifty years of separation from the family of the body have broken the identification.

I have no means of knowing whether there were any effects, beneficial or otherwise, from what I felt myself caused to do. Even if my now deceased mother's perceptions were correct, I can reasonably doubt that the victim was aware of what was happening.

However, the story illustrates so many aspects of the subject of past lives, even allowing for the fragility of the evidence, that it is worth telling.

A point that should be brought out is that the wish for revenge on the part of the murdered man was almost certainly not the cause of the ancestor's death. The murdered man could not himself kill, but as a disembodied spirit he had access to the 'spread of time' greater than that available to living people, and he could see that the ancestor would probably die at Ticonderoga. He could only wait for the already fated death with vengeance in his heart. His ill will, combined with his murderer's guilt, would help to turn a possibility into a certainty.

10

Big Dreams

'Big dreams' are generally less concerned with the dreamer's personal psychology than they are with instructing him in matters concerning the human state, man's relation to the universe, cosmology, and matters of this sort.

Such 'instructions' can cover anything from insights into a political system whose principles and policies are antagonistic to the spiritual evolution of mankind, to being given a taste of the mystical unity of being. It is, therefore, difficult to find examples which adequately illustrate the nature of these dreams. A published example is the case of Black Elk, a Sioux Indian who, at the age of nine, had an intense dream about the fate of his tribe. He could not understand it until elder members of the tribe helped him to enact it in ritual form.[1]

The following account of an Indian woman's dream illustrates how socially imposed feelings of guilt may inhibit or conflict with a person's spiritual aspirations. In this case, although an individual's guilt is being dealt with, the issue is cosmological in its significance.

---

[1] *Black Elk Speaks*, John G. Neihardt (ed.); William Morrow & Co., 1932.

She saw that a sadhu, who was a devotee of Sri Krishna, had died and was brought before Yama Raj, the judge of the dead. Sri Krishna, the object of the sadhu's worship, was present.

Yama Raj, as he must, read out from his book the list of the sadhu's good and evil deeds. The evil predominated, so Yama Raj sentenced him to take birth again where he would suffer the appropriate consequences. The sadhu appealed to Sri Krishna: 'I am your devotee. I have worshipped you and served you. You must save me from this fate.' For it is the teaching that the Lord protects his devotees.

Asked by Sri Krishna whether he had actually done these deeds, the sadhu admitted that he had. 'Then you must submit to Yama Raj's judgement, I can do nothing,' said Sri Krishna. And no matter how much his devotee pleaded, Krishna remained firm. The sadhu must return to birth.

Suddenly light dawned on him in his despair. 'No!' he cried. 'I have done none of these things, neither the bad nor the good. It is you and you alone who did them.' And with this realization that the individual is but the vehicle of the divine will, the sadhu passed beyond Yama Raj and his wheel of fate.

It is clear that this drama and its outcome was relevant to the lady's own concern with events in her past which Indian mores condemned as sinful. If not reconciled, the sense of guilt could have held her under the control of the lower aspect of the Self (symbolized in the dream as Yama Raj), instead of her being free to pass beyond the dualities of good and bad to the greater truth of the unity of being—a truth which can be found only after egotistic motives have been transcended.

What is the meaning of Yama Raj and similar judges of

the dead? From where come the criteria for the judgements of right and wrong, and what is the nature of the power which sends the soul back to birth? Do good deeds liberate the soul from rebirth? According to the Upanishads and again in the vision of Er recounted at the end of Plato's *Republic*, good deeds give one a pleasant period after death and bad deeds give an unpleasant time: but in both cases one returns to birth. Then what liberates? What is 'Krishna' and how is it that seeing him as the performer of actions frees the devotee from the cycle of birth and death?

Visions of this sort raise such questions which should be pondered till answers come—answers which may unveil further mysteries and give further liberation from the bonds of conventional thinking. Always the emphasis falls on the importance of asking the right questions and not resting until the answers come. If the answers were to be written down here and passively taken in to the reader's mind, there would be no liberating effect.

From the Mahabharata's Yaksha (a wonderful being) which traps the Pandava brothers with its questions which only Yudhishthira, the eldest brother, can answer, to the questions of the Greek Sphinx, throughout all the mythologies of the world the importance of the right answers is stressed. In contrast, one of the legends of King Arthur illustrates the importance of asking the right question at the right time. After much journeying, one of the knights finds the mysterious castle of the Holy Grail and fights his way into it. Then the maidens of the castle bathe him, dress his wounds, array him in fine garments and lead him to the banqueting hall. In the middle of the banquet, a hush falls on the company as a procession sweeps through the hall, bearing strange symbols. When it has passed and nothing more happens, the company returns to its feasting. After the banquet the knight is led to a splendid bedchamber, and he sleeps.

When he wakes in the morning, he is lying on the ground; the castle with its knights and mysteries has disappeared. The opportunity for the enlightenment he fought for has come to nothing because he did not demand to be told the meaning of that procession, that mystery which had been shown.

Too many of us are like that knight: we allow our visions to pass before our eyes and do not force them to give up their secrets. If the truth be told, we fear to ask lest the answers show us the falsity of the security we believe our physical existence gives us.

There is an additional significance to this fear of direct inquiry. We are inquiring at the root of the actual mystery, where any answer there is will be found. This is to be contrasted with the indirect inquiry, which entails the study of what others have said about it and the practices they have recommended, an inquiry that is frequently associated with the search for a teacher. It is a safe, socially approved search. The consequence of this is that, instead of looking for whatever it is that may be there, people look to find it in the form of a preconceived image deriving from what someone has said about it. Then, instead of allowing the awakened Self to guide him to a teacher in whom the Seeker can recognize the qualities of the Self who resides in his own heart, he goes hunting for a guru whom he measures by the standards of his conscious mind—his learning, his looks, his popularity, his social status—and he will be fortunate if he is not cheated.

In another 'big dream', a Seeker found himself in a marshy lake that seemed to be the source of the Brahmaputra river in Tibet. He was floating on his back, with his head to the south and with his gaze fixed on a star in the northern sky. He was caught by the strong current at the lake's outlet and carried away head first to the south. While he watched the star, the river carried him swiftly downstream until he reached the estuary in the Bay of Bengal. There he was carried under the surface of the sea, losing sight of the star. Finally he was brought to the surface, still facing the direction from which he had come. There, shining in the northern sky before him was the same star he had watched from the moment he had left the river's source in Tibet. Only for that short interval between his reaching the estuary and his coming to the surface in the sea had it disappeared.

The key to the dream lies, of course, in the meaning of the word *Brahmaputra*, the 'son of Brahma', son of Absolute Being. As a river, the Brahmaputra is factually one of the great rivers of the world, fittingly symbolizing the immense outpouring of the creative flow which gives birth to gods, worlds and men, as it thunders through the Himalayan gorges from the highlands of Tibet to the Indian plains, and so on to the ocean of existence.

With that flow we are brought to birth. As we enter birth we forget the memory not only of previous lives but also of our origin—a forgetting that is here symbolized by the plunge below the ocean. The same forgetting was represented in Greek mythology by the souls having to drink from the river Lethe, the waters of forgetfulness.

The Seeker, who at all times is trying to hold his awareness of the divinity within his heart and who knows that more lives will be needed for him to complete the course, is concerned at the compulsive plunge into forgetfulness that comes with each new birth. This vision shows him that constantly holding his attention on the Self, symbolized by the star, ensures that the memory of the Self will return to him in the form of self-awareness as soon as he gets his head above the surface of the ocean of life in the world. The continuity of the inner effort is thus assured.

My last example of a 'big dream' comes from the life of a high court lawyer. He had been brought up in an orthodox family, a Brahmin, well-read in both Indian and Western philosophy and arrogant in his knowledge. His family background was Shakta, the worship of the goddess, with a heavy emphasis on the utter transcendentalism of the Advaita philosophy according to which the world is an illusion and without meaning or purpose—except to the extent that man sees the illusion and so wins freedom from it by losing himself in the source from which he came.

However, as is often the case with Bengalis, he had a strong 'feeling' side which had led him to my guru, Sri Krishna Prem, whose spiritual quest had as its bedrock a compassionate view of the universe, approximately corresponding to what is known as the Bodhisattva doctrine. In this view, the world is still an illusion, in the sense that it is not what it appears to be—solid lumps of matter floating in time and space. However, it is a meaningful illusion, pervaded by love, through which the undifferentiated source of all being becomes aware of the multifold qualities that inhere in it. These concealed qualities or potentialities become separated and objectifiable or knowable when differentiated in the creative outpouring. That source—'He', 'She', 'It', 'That', no pronoun is adequate to describe it—requires a vehicle through which the perception of its qualities in manifestation can take place. Without such a vehicle, the source would remain ignorant of its own nature.

This vehicle is Man—the aware and self-aware being

through whose eyes THAT sees everything: sees and joys in being.

The individualized self of man is, therefore, of dual significance: looking inwards, Man discovers his identity with the Source of all things. Looking outwards through Man's eyes, the unmanifest Source knows itself in manifestation.

Like almost everyone, the lawyer whose 'big dream' is under discussion had some deeply rooted fixed ideas: in dreams one may find these symbolized by teeth—the hardest concretions in the body. When such ideas are sound, they can be extremely valuable—no one would want to extract a sound tooth. But if they happen to be false, they can badly distort the person's aims. Once their falsity is seen, their removal is usually easy. The difficulty lies in seeing their falsity. Frequently this is because such fixed ideas belong to a hallowed tradition whose sanctity inhibits the sort of rational criticism which would question its validity.

In this case, the fixed idea was the doctrine that the highest human aim is the liberation of the individual from the wheel of birth and death, in a manner that annihilates both the individual and any possible consequences of his experience of annihilation. Nothing remains, nothing is changed, and the universe continues exactly as it was before.

The sanctity of this view is hallowed by a thousand years of Advaita which has inspired countless Indian Seekers; and that is why our friend could not see the inconsistency between his acceptance of his guru's vision of a universe pervaded by love, and his simultaneously holding to a doctrine which, in the context, appears as a bloodless denial of love.

One night he 'dreamed' of the Void—a vast and empty blackness. Far away a glowing mist was blown out from a point—a mist he knew was the creative outpouring, the outbreathing of Brahma. It swirled out into the darkness, turning back on itself to enclose a dark space in the shape of a womb. Within that womb a child began to form.

Out of that cosmic womb the child took birth. But the child was stillborn—dead. The enormous effort of the manifestation had given birth to Man. But Man had refused the trust laid upon him. He had refused the burden of becoming the perfected or completed vehicle through whom alone the divine being might find himself. The purpose of the creation could not be fulfilled. At the moment that the whole cycle of evolution was completed, and Man was born as a perfected being, he lost his manhood and succumbed to the selfish bliss of self loss. He had merely returned to the Source.

In another image of the same theme, the World Tree produces one of its rare flowers. As the flower opens, it drops to the ground. The beauty of that golden flower will not shine out over our dark universe unless the individual accepts the suffering and responsibility which are the price of love.

The wonder of the vision had carried our friend away, but the shock of that stillborn child was too much for him, for he was essentially a soft-hearted man. We heard no more of the bliss of self-annihilation.

This last point emphasizes one of the most important aspects of the interpretation of 'big dreams' and, indeed, of many lesser ones. This is the impact of the images themselves upon the dreamer.

In translating symbols into words, we often risk the danger of depotentizing the image, turning it into an intellectual concept and so diminishing its power to continue to affect the dreamer. For such an image has an inherent wealth of meaning which will unfold only over a long period of time.

Our interpretation must not restrict its significance to a single meaning, even if we believe that to be the most important one. As in our example of the Brahmaputra river, its significance cannot be encompassed merely by calling it 'The River of Life'.

11

Death Dreams

Among prognostic dreams, death dreams are perhaps the commonest; at least they are the most commonly remembered. But there are also dreams and apparitions of the recently dead which, since they often convey the first news to the recipient, can be counted in with those warning of death, which come more often to relations and friends than to the person who will die.

From the death dreams I have seen and heard of, it appears as if each culture has specific death symbols which regularly appear in dream. In the Christian West, for example, the horse often symbolizes death, especially when associated with the Pale Horse on which Death rides in the *Revelations of St. John* in the Bible. As with all the historical religions, however, one may reasonably suspect that the horse as a symbol of death may long pre-date the religion to which it has become attached.

In the 1930s, an Englishwoman in India confided that she was trying to resolve her marital troubles because she felt her inner growth depended on it. Then, after returning to England, she dreamed she was marking out a tennis court, and was fixing the iron right-angles which were used to mark the corners on a grass court. She had fixed three, but was having trouble with the fourth. As she struggled with it, a calm-eyed rider on a horse came up, and the horse stamped the angle into place.

She died shortly afterwards. It would seem that the last part of her personal problem could be resolved only by death. In Jungian terms, the tennis court was a Mandala, and the effort was to integrate the psyche with the completion of the rectangle, which, as two squares joined together, would represent the two persons of the married relationship.

Another example of the horse as a dream symbol for death came from an old theosophist living in Glasgow. After many years of correspondence, he wrote of a dream in which a horse reared up against him. This was his last letter.

Throughout history, the symbol of the horse has been strongly connected with the libido and the life force. When this turns against one, death ensues. As the first example shows, however, death is by no means always seen as an enemy. Indeed, in Europe, Death is also known as the 'pale sweetheart'.

In India, death symbols include the black dog, the wedding procession, the old widow who smiles on one, and the howling of jackals.

The wedding procession, with its celebrations, symbolizes the joyful reunion of the person with his higher Self. I have known several instances of such a dream being taken as a sign of impending death, which has come within the next six months.

A black dog is often referred to as *Kal Bhairav*—a terror-striking form of Shiva. There is also a pun on *kal* as time and *kala* as black. The black dog is also seen as the messenger of Yama Raj, Lord of Death and judge of the dead. His messengers, often seen as black and rather devilish figures, are sent to fetch the people due to die, forcibly carrying them out of their bodies. Dying people sometimes see them as if hanging around, waiting for the right moment. And folklore is full of stories of the messengers carrying off the wrong man, usually of the same name as the person who should have died (in the villages, one may know twenty Ram Singhs in the area) who has had to be returned—if the body has not already been cremated.

An elderly Gujarati widow told me her husband had appeared in dream and warned her to get ready to join him. Then she dreamed that a black dog jumped up at her in play (in real life, this particular black dog, because of her colour, was called Yami—the wife of Yama Raj.) She died in less than three months.

Two months before Sri Krishna Prem died, I dreamed that the temple images were broken—the images being the forms in which the deity resides and through which he is worshipped, just as the guru's physical body is the form through which the disciple serves the Lord in serving the guru. In the same situation I dreamed that the sun was setting.

Then there was the period in the 1950s when a very dear friend, a much older man who treated me as a son, was slowly dying in Calcutta from a series of strokes. From about eighteen months before he died, I had a series of premonitory dreams in which a municipal sweeper in rags was pushing one of the light, four-wheeled trolleys used by the Calcutta municipality for the removal of dead bodies. The sweeper was dancing in the street called Freeschool Street, and slowly moving in the general direction of my friend's dwelling. The same scene was repeated several times at intervals of months, each time the sweeper's dance becoming faster and more furious.

My friend was in Calcutta, and I was in my guru's ashram

in the UP hills. One morning I was idly observing a cracked and stained whitewashed wall with whose patterns I was familiar, and familiar, too, with the images the psyche will often build out of the matrix of dots and lines. On this occasion, however, I was surprised to see an unfamiliar picture. Clearly shown, and withstanding blinking and shaking of the head, was my friend's form. Furthermore, he was dressed exactly as he invariably was for the eighteen-mile journey from and to Almora by footpath on the days he arrived at and left the ashram, and on no other days (for this journey he wore his old university Cadet Corps breeches).

A few minutes later I was outside the open door of the temple kitchen where Sri Krishna Prem was cooking. I told him what I had just seen, with the unspoken suggestion that this might mean he had left his body. My guru then told me that he himself had just seen our friend's face in the cracked mud plaster of a wall just outside the kitchen door. The suggestion became a certainty, confirmed a day or two later when the telegram arrived.

This same mode of 'seeing' a recently deceased person happened to me again when I saw the face of another Bengali who had great respect and affection for Sri Krishna Prem though he had never visited the ashram. It was in the evening, and Sri Krishna Prem was singing devotional hymns, Bengali kirtan, in the temple, as was his practice, while I accompanied him. I saw this friend's face in the folds of the cloth in which the temple images were clothed. Singing with his eyes closed, my guru saw nothing. On this occasion we had no knowledge that our friend was ill, let alone dying. The letter from his widow came some days later.

As another example of a fairly long-term warning of death, I can tell the story of something that happened in 1954 when my guru and I were staying in Banaras with the younger brother of Yashoda Mai, my guru's deceased guru. Now in his sixties, he had lived a rather wild life, slightly held in check by his very real respect, amounting to devotion, for his famous sister. He was beginning to have serious heart trouble.

One morning when we went to meet our 'uncle' (*mama*) we found him still, moved by a vision he had had on waking. Two women sannyasins had entered his room, dressed in the ochre robes of their order. But he could not see their faces, and therefore could not recognize them. He felt sure that one of them was his sister, but he could not guess at the identity of the other. Inhibited by the hierarchical order of Bengali society, where degrees of respect are determined by age and seniority, he had never seen that Moti Rani (his elder sister's youngest daughter, who had died three years before and who had taken sannyas), hid behind her teasing manner a person of rare spiritual attainment. My guru's private comment to me was: 'When he sees their faces, he will go.'

He died in Calcutta, two years later. When he wrote to me, asking me to bring Sri Krishna Prem to see him, that warning made us go at once, and we stayed some four months until he died in my guru's presence.

The simplest explanation for this sort of vision is the straight one: that his sister and niece were able to appear to him with a warning of his impending death, and to do it when Krishna Prem, his sister's first disciple and her successor, was there to understand the message and to take appropriate action, such as being with him for several hours every day during the last four months of his life. The sort of psychological explanation of such events that appeals to the archetype of the Self, but then says that saints have no reality in themselves, is a distortion of fact in the interest of an ultimately materialistic theory.

Another experience dating from this same four-month period in Calcutta, though it deals with matters that are customarily told only to the guru, seemed to have been given with the intention that it should be told—or so my guru instructed me.

We had three dear and respected friends lying ill in the same town, all due to die, and all suffering: one was the same uncle suffering from a bad heart, one was paralysed by a stroke, and the third was a little old lady of ninety-six who, becoming dizzy from the effects of a religious fast, had sat down too quickly and broken her femur. The doctors of the day had nothing to offer.

I felt very strongly that their suffering was in some way unnecessarily prolonged, perhaps because they were unwilling to let go of their hold on life, or because they did not know how to let go. None of them was in the position of the Western materialist who clings to life in the body because he believes there is no life beyond it. If they could let go of the attachments which were holding them in their bodies, then their suffering would be minimal, and not this long drawn-out, unhappy affair, waiting for increasing pain to drive them out.

For me it was a frustrating situation. What I was feeling seemed so right; yet I had no experience to back it. Also, in the eyes of these elderly friends, I was a healthy youngster in my thirties, my guru's acolyte. There was nothing in my position to suggest to these traditionally-minded elders that they might take me seriously. 'Young man, we are suffering. You are not. What do you know about it!' would be the sort of reply I might expect. However, at that point in time it was a subliminal worry, and I had not framed my problem clearly enough to ask Sri Krishna Prem about it.

In mosquito-ridden Calcutta we slept under mosquito nets. One morning I woke knowing, as one does know in such situations, that my last breath was leaving me. I was dying. Yet there was not the slightest struggle for another breath, no pain, no fear. As the breath left me, I rose out of my body, through the mosquito net, and up to the angle where wall meets ceiling. There I woke fully, looked back at my body on the bed, and slammed back into it.

The event could be described as a simple etheric projection, of the sort many people are familiar with. The major difference between this sort of projection and death is that at death one does not return to the body. So there are grounds for the argument that I was not afraid because it was not death. However, it is only fair to add that I had practised 'dying', because it is only by dying a little that one can enter deep states of meditation.

The point of the event does not lie in the mechanism of etheric or astral projection—something with which I was, in any case, familiar. The leaving of the body being the same as at death, what was emphasized was that one can leave without struggle, without pain, without fear, and in full consciousness. I had been shown that to this extent what I had been feeling was true.

Telling Sri Krishna Prem about it the same morning I could now frame my problem. But since my private experience would not alter our friends' opinion of me, any use he might make of it had to be left to him.

In the event, the old lady was the first to go. After some ten days of complaining, 'Why should this happen to me!', she suddenly changed. 'Now I understand,' she said. 'The Lord's call has come.' In the manner of people of her day, she stopped eating and stopped medication. About a fortnight later she slipped away, gently and with dignity, with her great-grandson holding her hand.

The next was our uncle with a bad heart, suffering all the troubles heart patients had before modern medicine brought alleviation. It was only at around four in the afternoon that on some days he would feel well enough to meet his friends who would quietly affirm their friendship by playing bridge on the veranda in case he felt like joining them. Since he was not staying in his own house, he one day gave me his keys to fetch him some clothes from where we were staying. Having brought the clothes, I returned the keys. 'Your keys,' I said. He let them lie in the palm of his hand. '*My* keys,' he said with feeling. 'Even now, *my* keys.' And he tossed those symbols of possession onto the floor.

A day or two later he developed a bad toothache, and because of his heart condition the dentist could do nothing. It seemed to be the last straw. 'I can't keep this body any longer,' he told Sri Krishna Prem.

Two days later we arrived at our usual time to find him just woken from his afternoon sleep. We went to sit with him, I gently massaging his back in a way he liked while Sri Krishna Prem talked to him. Suddenly a heart attack started. While his wife frantically telephoned for the doctor, we watched a body seeming to struggle for breath. The man himself had already left.

The contrast between this man's attitude and that of our paralysed friend was remarkable. He was bedridden but well cared for. One hand was clenched by the stroke in a way that seemed to symbolize his hold on life. One could open the hand by gentle massage, but it soon closed again. 'Take me to the ashram,' he pleaded. 'I shall get well there.' But when Sri Krishna Prem tried to talk him into a more realistic state of mind and to face the facts of his condition, he would call for the urine bottle, which was equivalent to telling us to go.

It was another six months before another stroke took him off.

These three people illustrate so well three different ways of meeting—or not meeting—death. The old lady with her traditional acceptance, expressed in her fasting. The heart patient with his direct understanding of the need to let go when the body's condition became intolerable. And our paralysed friend, desperately clutching at life to the last moment.

When a person is truly liberated from the compulsions of the world's desires, then only will he not be compelled to take birth again. Liberation in these terms does not imply that the person must then proceed to self-annihilation in the Source from which all things have come. That is only one possibility among others.

However, the question for so many people in the modern world is not about alternative after-death states, but whether there is any after-death state of any sort at all. An important factor that may be mentioned here is that the human psyche takes no cognizance of death because it knows (and who should know better) that it does not die. This could explain why more prognostic death dreams come to friends and relatives than to the person to whom the dreams refer.

Religious teachings on the subject seem to have very little practical relevance. Only too often I have been approached by strangers who have begun by reading me a lecture on what their particular religions teach about death and reincarnation or heaven worlds. It all sounds very good, and they certainly know their stuff. But then they say with a hint of fear in their voices, 'But Swamiji, *is it true?*'

People who have had contact with the occult schools—spiritualists, theosophists, anthroposophists—appear to be better off in the face of death, perhaps because many of them have had first-hand experience of astral projection and various forms of communication with the dead, such that they have an image of what death may hold in store for them, once they have got past the awkward business of leaving the body. There may still be uncertainty, and there may not be much in the way of anything one might justly call spiritual—spiritualist, perhaps—but they do have some sort of support either from personal experience or from that of someone whom they trust.

Throughout Asia, China and Japan, and wherever one finds tribal and peasant societies, there are large numbers of people who are factually ancestor- or ghost-worshippers, no matter what their nominal religion may be. Through shamans or shaman-like priests they obtain guidance from the spirits about affairs that concern them—crops, weather, illness, business. They may also contract with the spirits for the discomfiture of their enemies, and for protection against their enemies' attacks.

In respect of death, such people have a very different problem from that of the materialist unbeliever. They are quite sure that the spirit world is real—often uncomfortably real. Any fear of death they have has nothing to do with the threat of annihilation, which is what bothers the materialist, but comes from the threat of harassment by the spirits, especially if they have been exploited for revenge against enemies. When these quite real spirits get mixed up with the frightening figures that rise up from the unconscious to be projected into the figures of dream, one gets a situation that is not very different from the ancient pictures of hell.

More fortunate people in these cultures may experience their particular form of heaven. A widow belonging to the Hindu reform movement (called the Brahmo Samaj) was dying, looked after by her daughter whom I had known for many years. The mother appeared to go into a death-like coma, but she came back to consciousness, joyfully telling her daughter that her husband had taken her to see where they would be living together—an archetypal Bengali village with bamboo and thatch huts, plenty of greenery, 'tanks' of clear water, cows and ducks. An hour or two later she passed away happily.

It appears as if the collective consciousness of such cultures creates these seemingly concrete images in representation of the cultural ideals of how people could live in peace and prosperity. How long such collective 'dreams' may last is anyone's guess.

When the Western materialist dismisses such accounts as superstitious nonsense, he forgets that he has nothing to put in their place, and that that is why he cannot face death with equanimity. The people who experience these heavens and hells may indeed be simple-minded and superstitious, but what they experience is a psychic reality—a shared reality, which, after all, is what *this* world is. Such after-death states are not mere illusions which ease the person's transition from embodied existence to nothingness. Those 'people' are surviving and will shortly return to birth in other bodies, just as the materialist will survive. What one believes may affect the sort of experience one will have, but it cannot alter facts.

In India it is evident that a great change took place in the attitude towards death with the introduction of modern medicine. One may assume that similar changes took place elsewhere in the same context. It was easier to adopt an accepting attitude towards the inevitability of death when the limitations of local medicines were well known and there was neither rapid transport nor rapid communications to carry sick people from rural areas to city centres. The introduction of air travel also affected the manner in which dying parents would cling to life while a beloved son flew home from America, and families preserved bodies on ice so that relations living far away could come to look their last on the body.

All this goes to show how shallow the effects of religious teaching can be. In the old world, many were the people who, in the last stages of an illness that was felt to be terminal, would stop eating and leave the body with dignity; the family would normally support such a decision. But the moment the opportunity for prolonging life is offered, the very idea of fasting is abandoned, and not reverted to even when modern treatment fails.

The rapid disposal of dead bodies which was customary, often within an hour or two of death, was not merely because of rapid decomposition in a hot climate, but importantly from a genuine perception that the person had gone; what was left was merely 'earth', to be disposed of as quickly as possible. Yet the moment refrigeration became available, this high detachment from sentimentality could not hold against the down-dragging pulls of family fixations. As Sri Krishna Prem pointed out, 'In the West they say "The Spirit left him", or "He gave up the ghost". In India we say "He left the body".' It is not only for the population explosion that we have to thank Western medicine; it is also for the degradation of the Indian spirit. Yet we all know that had that spirit been truly integrated, those fine perceptions that the individual's significance does not lie in the body would not have crumbled so easily.

What, in fact, is the dominant Western attitude towards death, which spreads to every country touched by materialism? As I have already suggested, religious teachings and beliefs are not really the point, for all too many people might still give the same reply to the question of what they believe happens after death, as that of the London club gentleman between the wars: 'Of course we go to heaven and enjoy eternal bliss. But need we discuss such an unpleasant subject?' Indeed, one gets the impression that thousands of people lie suffering in hospitals, living from crisis to crisis, not because the law is against alternatives but because their world view provides no space for non-physical existence and a meaningful evolution of the individual soul through the accumulation of experience in many lives.

And so there has to be suffering, driving people to understand that, while one can have great pleasure and enjoyment in life, life itself is not for pleasure. Life's purpose is beyond itself.

Some doctors in hospices, caring for people with terminal illnesses beyond the reach of medicine, have testified to learning much about dying from watching their patients go through the stages of anger, resentment, and despair—and sometimes into a calm acceptance of death as a transition. Sometimes the patients find, or are helped to find, a deep level within their beings which knows that life does not end.

Often enough, there are remarkable consequences to this finding of the deep level. High drug dosages, barely controlling the pain, may be dropped to half. Or the attitude to pain becomes so changed that the pain becomes manageable. There is no theorizing here; theory follows to fit the facts. In the face of these demonstrations of the power of consciousness, what is to be gained by repeating the old lie that all things are material, and that when the brain dissolves into a putrescent liquid consciousness disappears? The Hindu *Mahavakya* (great saying) is more to the point: 'All is Brahma.'

These last-minute conversions just happen to be facts. However, wonderful though they are, I am not recommending them. I am not the only person to have realized that that remarkable text, *The Tibetan Book of the Dead*, supposed to be chanted over the body of a dying or dead man and to ensure his liberation from rebirth, or at least from an unfortunate birth, is best understood as a text for a lifetime's study, a *sadhana*, which will only bear fruit at death. So it is with the development of any conscious attitude towards dying, if it is to prove effective. One must spend many years struggling to make sense of a seemingly purposeless life, and seeking to isolate, identify and to enhance that strange power of self-awareness which lies at the root of our beings and is the central essence of all that survives the death of the body.

On the other side of the coin there are still plenty of simple, straightforward people whose feelings for the Saints, Mahatmas, or Gurus carries them through the events of their lives and the final event of death; for is not devotion a form of love, and is not love the key to the whole mystery?

At another place in these notes on dreams I have referred to the importance of stilling the mind so as to get beyond it—perhaps to that same 'deep level' of which some hospice doctors speak. (One hesitates to make equations, because there are so many levels of being. Also, the 'same' level seems to alter according to the attitude of the person entering it.) I have also referred to the need for 'dying a little' in order to enter deep states of meditation.

In this last case, what is it that dies? The ego-centred

integration. Whatever it is that holds the view: this is for *me*, for *my* use, *my* pleasure, *my* gain. The thing that wants to be safe, secure, comfortable, loved, cared for. The thing that wants to go out, conquer, achieve, win approval, prove itself. The thing which feels: this body *is me*. I belong to this family, this nationality, this group. I am this person with these characteristics, these educational qualifications, these abilities—all the things which allow me to run a business, to hold a job, earn money, compete with others, show off my spending power. The thing that does not want to look to where it is all going—to death.

This ego, this thing with its ambitions and self-assertiveness, is what provides for most people the reason for living. This is why getting rid of it and its trash feels like dying. When one lets go of all these ephemeral aims and self-evaluations, and one faces those urgent desires which have been driving them, then only can the mind go calm and clear, like the pure waters of a mountain lake. Then, too, one knows that death holds nothing to fear. Free from anxieties and inhibitions, one may perform one's worldly activities even better than before, if they seem worth doing at all. And when the time allotted to this body has run its course, one can leave without a struggle and, if necessary, return without fear.

I must not end this chapter on death dreams without sounding a warning to dream interpreters. If the danger I speak of is recorded in books, I have not come across them. I had to learn the hard way by making a fool of myself, hopefully without harming the person concerned.

An ageing Gujarati lady approached me with her dreams, which seemed to be death dreams. One of the items was of threats from buffaloes, which are another of the Indian death symbols—sometimes.

One should never tell anyone, least of all a simple old lady, that dreams clearly predict death. It might be kinder to kill her immediately. On the other hand, when her own dreams appear to be warning her, one has no right to conceal the fact. It is a difficult situation, calling for much tact and consideration.

The dreams continued, and though this made me uneasy, for the repetition of a theme often means that one has failed to find the correct interpretation, I could see no other meaning. The lady seemed unperturbed by the thought of death, so if this was what the dreams were saying, who was I to deny it? I wrote to her relations that they should be forewarned. The dreams continued—and so did the old lady. That was twenty years ago and she is still happily alive. It was only after a couple of years had passed that I learned from her granddaughter what she herself had concealed from me, that many years earlier some irresponsible fool of an astrologer had told her she would certainly die at sixty-five— the age at which she had started having death dreams. I had not spotted that anxiety arising from such a suggestion could produce these dreams. Fortunately, the prediction did not become a self-fulfilling prophecy.

12

Great Beings

In this chapter we are concerned with the nature of dream experience in which Great Beings give teaching on matters which are relevant to the spiritual path itself, rather than to the ground-clearing operations of ordinary psychological dreams. We must, therefore, affirm that the path we are travelling is real, the attainment is real, and that some of those who have attained remain in the subtle worlds in order to help others.

So long as we were concerned only with the interpretation of dreams, we did not need to consider the degrees of reality there may be in what we see in the world of dream. But when the mirror of dream, which reflects the messages of the psyche, becomes the window of vision, we have to come to terms with the fact that there are real entities inhabiting real subtle worlds, beyond that of our everyday normal waking consciousness.

In the same sense that in the world of waking experience we can be 'asleep', carrying out our daily business automatically, without self-awareness; we can be day-dreaming, our minds filled with fantasy; and we can be 'awake' as self-conscious beings; so in the world of dream we can be sound asleep with no mental activity; we can be dreaming, watching the images thrown on the screen of dream by the psyche; and we can be awake, as in astral projection, seeing both the world of waking experience exactly as it appears in the ordinary waking state, and the subtle world itself.

There are no hard and fast divisions. They overlap, one running into the other, as we described in the chapter on out-of-the-body dreams.

All the work on dream analysis, which has previously been described, taken along with meditation and other exercises, is designed to heighten self-awareness. Heightened self-awareness enhances the degree of awakeness one can maintain in both the worlds. The more awake one is, the more one understands the nature of the ordinary waking world, and the more one can distinguish between dream images and the reality which underlies them.

The question of there being real entities in the subtle worlds is a highly controversial subject. Firstly, we have the materialists who deny the existence of subtle worlds and so of entities that might inhabit them. Such people will also deny that there is any spiritual attainment to be achieved, and even psychical phenomena will be treated as fraudulent, something that would be exposed as fraud if the person producing them was stripped naked. Then we have the psychologist Jung, who relegated visions of saints and similarly Great Beings to the limbo of his 'Archetypes of the Collective Unconscious' which, he says, are real only in the sense of being real human experiences, but have no objective reality—though his views on ghosts were later changed by his experience in a haunted house during a stay in England. Then there are people who seem able to believe that Tom, Dick and Harry may have some sort of after-life existence, but sneer at the idea of disembodied Mahatmas such as the

Masters whom Madame Blavatsky writes about. And there are a lot of people who would agree with the French Contesse who, asked if she believed in ghosts, is supposed to have replied, 'No! But I am frightened of them.' Indeed, those who deny the reality of the subtle worlds lie under the suspicion of denying them because they are childishly afraid of 'spooks'.

There remain a large number of people, even in the developed world, who firmly believe in the real existence of subtle worlds, the dead who inhabit them, and in the Saints, Mahatmas, Gurus, Perfected Men and Bodhisattvas who, though essentially formless, adopt form for the sake of foolish human beings who would not know they were there if they could not see them. Of course, 'firm beliefs' are often besieged by doubts until personal experience puts its seal on them.

Secondly, we should try to understand who or what these Great Beings are. They are men and women who, by extraordinary effort, have reached the term of human evolution and found the identity of their individual selves with the universal self—what is often called God. Having transcended any sense of egotistic separateness from the Divinity, they are at-one with Him. It is said that God then looks out through their eyes at the world, sees, understands and joys in His own manifest form.

But this is only a partial description. In what one may call the ordinary course of events, the person who experienced the bliss of that union of the individual self with the universal self blends utterly with the universal self and is lost to this world (see the 'big dream' of the still-born child in Chapter 10). However, there is another path, characterized by love and the acceptance of the suffering that goes with love, in which the person in Bodhisattva-like compassion, dedicates himself to remaining in contact with the world in order to help others reach the same goal. These are the Saints, Mahatmas, Gurus, Masters and Bodhisattvas, whose state of being is indescribable.

A point that needs noting here is that these Great Beings are not to be equated with the traditional saints of all the religions. Some may be, but many are relatively unknown persons who quietly pursued their path outside any conventional religion, and attained.

One of the ways in which these Great Beings help mankind is by giving teaching through the medium of dream—often 'big dreams'—in which the dreamer feels himself to be in the presence of an utterly real person of tremendous character. This is quite unlike the ordinary dream where the figures are more like cardboard cut-outs than real people.

When the Bodhisattva appears in dream or vision, the impact may be so great that any doubts the dreamer might have had are overwhelmed. The reality of the Bodhisattva himself and the validity of his message come across with such certainty that he can ignore his knowledge that the Bodhisattva's form is an illusory appearance, a cognizance adopted for the sake of being recognized by the dreamer, and that the images in which the message is clothed may, like most dream images, have no material existence, or may be built up from the images stored in memory.

It is to the point to contrast this dream experience of the Bodhisattva with the dreams any disciple may have in which his personal guru or teacher appears. In most such cases, the living guru will seldom admit to having any knowledge of the dream. He himself has played no part in it. The figure in the dream is not him, but a representation of what the guru means to the disciple.

A word of warning has to be added. Enormously encouraging though such interventions may be, they must be accepted with great humility. It is only too easy for the dreamer to swell with pride at this proof of his progress, and then be unable to resist hinting to his friends that the Bodhisattvas came to him, with the unspoken assumption that they came because he is so advanced. It is more likely that they came to him to help master his ego.

When the Bodhisattva gives teaching through dreams, it is akin to the dreamer being shown a drama that has been prepared beforehand. If the figure of the Bodhisattva appears in the dream he may no more be actually present than in the case of the disciple dreaming of his guru. But this must not be taken to mean that he is never present, particularly when the aspirant has worked to be sufficiently awake in dream for it to be closer to a waking astral projection.

The subject is beset with traps for the unwary. Humility is the only safeguard—humility and the traditional teaching that inner experiences of this sort are to be shared only with one's guru. Indeed, the main purpose in describing some of the difficulties is to help avoid the trap of thinking oneself great because the Bodhisattva actually came to see one, or permitted one to see him. Apart from that, what difference does it make to the aspirant whether Bodhisattva X himself came, or whether he sent a packaged message to be delivered at his bedside. How many people who long for such contact with the Bodhisattvas are capable of telling the difference? What matters is that these Great Beings are utterly real, and that their compassion is so great that they may continue to help someone whose lack of humility would seem to make him unworthy.

13

Conclusion

Had I intended to write a handbook on dream analysis I would have had to fill out the text with many more examples of dreams, with analyses and comments. My purpose, however, is only to draw attention to a much-neglected aspect of dreams, which is the guidance to the spiritual aspirant which can come through them.

The neglect is, perhaps, partly due to the difficulty of dream interpretation, and also to the ease with which one can be deceived by false interpretations—and can deceive oneself. But one has to go deeper to find the main reasons.

Although psychology has done much to rescue dreaming from its degraded position as an unreliable form of divination, psychology in general, with the possible exception of schools deriving from Jung, gives no credence to the reality of the Spirit. Indeed, the materialism of the modern world view is reflected in the very high proportion of psychologists who practise as psychiatrists—i.e., who believe more in the power of drugs to effect changes in mental and emotional states than in the psychology of the unconscious, with its pursuit of the psychic causation of mental disturbance. In this context, it is not surprising that, as mentioned in the first chapter, many avowedly spiritual schools prefer to avoid psychology altogether.

A common attitude towards religion also has a bearing on this subject, in the way people tend to treat religion as a separate department of life. Visions are acceptable within religion, to the extent that their nature allows them to be ascribed to God and his prophets. But dreams are suspect because so many of them are openly sexual, as discussed earlier and are, therefore, apt to be ascribed by the major religions to the powers of darkness.

When religion is treated as a distinct department of life, then it is assumed that anything spiritual must belong exclusively to that department. Any mystical component within a religious society will know that the Spirit cannot be thus confined, but it is surprising how many otherwise intelligent and educated people have difficulty in accepting the presence of the Spirit in events which have no direct connection with the practices of a religion.

For example: when a friend of mine was giving a talk to police officers on the importance of adhering to standards of behaviour which ultimately derived from spiritual principles, an inspector general intervened with the remark that what was being said was all very good, but he could not see what bearing it had on practical police work. He said that his men were not religious—they did not go to temples, etc., or say their prayers—yet when his party was later ambushed by dacoits, two of his men saved his life at risk of their own.

The inspector general had not understood that what he presented as an objection was really an illustration in support of what my friend was saying, namely, that there are real values, natural to man as man and rooted in the very structure of the universe, whose validity is independent of the doctrine of any specific religion.

This does not answer all the questions that arise out of

the anecdote, as, for example, the relative merits of saving a dacoit from a policeman and saving an inspector general of police from dacoits. But the story does illustrate the difficulty felt by so many people in understanding how one can approach spiritual things through a direct inquiry into the roots of human awareness, quite independently of religious doctrine and its associated rules, rituals, and general mystifications. God and Spirit have been put into a separate compartment labelled 'religion'; anything outside that compartment is secular. This as often applies to people who think they have abandoned religion as it does to the faithful.

This difficulty has to be overcome if the human race is ever to win freedom from priest-ridden systems of religious belief and to find its way back to the Spirit that resides in everyman's heart. However, we can begin only with as many people as are now ready to grasp the concept and apply it to their lives. Few or many, they have need of guidance. Dream is everyman's guide.

Index

By the same author:

Man, the Measure of All Things (with Sri Krishna Prem) Rider & Co., London
Man, Son of Man, Rider & Co., London
Relating to Reality, Banyan Books, New Delhi

Books of related interest:

The Yoga of the Kathopanishad, Sri Krishna Prem, John M. Watkins, London
The Yoga of the Bhagavat Gita, Sri Krishna Prem, Stuart & Watkins, London
Initiation into Yoga, Sri Krishna Prem, B.I. Publications, New Delhi
Yogi Sri Krishnaprem, Dilip Kumar Roy, Bharatiya Vidya Bhavan, Mumbai
Guru By Your Bedside, S.D. Pandey, Penguin Books, New Delhi
Letters from Mirtola, written by Sri Krishna Prem and Sri Madhava Ashish to Karan Singh, Bharatiya Vidya Bhavan, Mumbai
In Search of the Unitive Vision, Seymour B. Ginsburg, New Paradigm Books, USA